Lewis Armstrong

BLACK NOSTRADAMUS PROPHECIES OF AMERICA'S FUTURE

LEWIS JEROME ARMSTRONG

authorHOUSE®

AuthorHouse™
1663 Liberty Drive
Bloomington, IN 47403
www.authorhouse.com
Phone: 1-800-839-8640

First published by AuthorHouse   11/19/2009

ISBN: 978-1-4490-3849-6 (e)
ISBN: 978-1-4490-3848-9 (sc)
ISBN: 978-1-4490-3847-2 (hc)

Printed in the United States of America
Bloomington, Indiana

This book is printed on acid-free paper.

CONTENTS

INTRODUCTION

The dictionary term prediction means to forecast an event of the future. The Holy Bible has complex religious teachings called the mysteries. Many areas of forecasting can be drawn from these teachings. Religious teaching or theology is a system of esoteric study. It can save individuals or nations from destruction. Careful study can show a person the future of a nation as he looks at events that have been written thousands of years ago. This book will give you a look into the predictions without showing where these predictions can be found. Esoteric study must be respected as sacred knowledge. Still, knowing the future is available to all of us. This book also gives the reader a chance to see a philosophy that has been overlooked by millions of churchgoers. Even in chapters like the one on the Seven Seals, you can see history of the past, present and future from the Revelator's day unfold before your eyes. You will be able to better understand Revelation 1:13-19 as you never have before. In addition, while reading the story of Joseph, seen through esoteric study, learn how God used prophets and writers to hide the truth from the eyes of the masses until the last days. In the coming days men and women will rise up and turn from the old ways that the gospel has been taught into a new, "show-me" attitude toward the study of religion. The book teaches its readers how not to put their faith in religious groups just because of church doctrine or because a church professes a love for Christ; but to put their trust in the spiritual and political leaders the Holy Bible says will come and lead you into esoteric truth. May God bless America through the troubling and difficult times to come!

ACKNOWLEDGMENTS

First, thanks to Almighty God, the Lord Jesus and the Holy Spirit, for inspiring me to write on the subject.

I thank my wife, Carole Vallee Armstrong, for being beside me through this much needed work; my deceased brother, Eddie Lee Armstrong, who talked to me about how this work and others would help people overcome this troubled world and place mankind on the right path.

I thank my sons and daughters for just making me want to succeed in this work for all Americans and others.

I thank God for all of my fathers before me, for they are who I am. I never want to take for granted mothers; so thank you, Essie Mae Armstrong, for being my mother.

PREFACE

This book, Black Nostradamus: Prophecies of America's Future is the culmination of many years of work in the study of the Holy Bible, gospel teaching and history, as well as years of studying esoteric and mythology. Research has played an important part in this work. The esoteric teaching of the Bible and other writings teaches that this is a duty and a religious responsibility to give these truths to mankind. In short, the purpose of this book is to help Americans and others understand God's words and recognize the Holy Bible as an instrument to teach all of us how to overcome the bad events that will threaten our existence.

BLACK NOSTRADAMUS
PROPHECIES OF AMERICA'S FUTURE

This book, "Black Nostradamus Prophecies of America's Future", and the book before this, "Judgment of America", have many truths inside its covers. I will cover some of the prophecies of my first published book that as you read you can see that these prophecies need to be considered. The Book Judgment of America was first published by Author House August 23, 2006. It ISBN is (1-4259-4163-X(sc) and 1-4259-4164-8(d j). When looking on page 127 of the book Judgment of America the thought of a black President was revealed and published before a large number of Americans ever heard or even thought of a Barack Obama for President. This thought came from Nostradamus Century 5, Quatrain 84, written by John Hogue's 1997 book, The Complete Prophecies. He wrote C5Q84, "He will be born of the gulf and unmeasured city, born of parents obscure and shadowy: he who the revered power of a great King will wish to destroy through Rouen and Eureaux". From this an idea of a black President came to mind. But this one wasn't Barack Obama. The person in this writing was the second president elected after Barack Obama. So I had to look in the Bible to find Obama and I did by finding his wife's name. At that time I saw that there was going to be three black Presidents elected in the USA. President Barack Obama is the first, then the one that is written in C5Q84. The next black President will have a son that will be the third black President of the USA. These three will be very important men in American history. The letter written to President Bush on September 24, 2003 which can be found on page 129-30 of the book, Judgment of America has a prophecy about his election in 2004. The very top of page 130 said to the President that he will have a next turn, not may be, but *will* have a next turn. Although many people wanted him out of the White House, history wanted him in. The same page speaks about George W. Bush's brother, Jeb Bush, considering a run for the White House. In 2006 he steps toward the White House and back down. Then in 2009 he said he's going to run for the senate seat and then to the White House but he backed down again. He did step toward the senator's seat, and back down making this prophecy 100% true. Also, on page 93, 94 of the book, Judgment of America, there is a prophetic chart of the economy as good, bad and grievously bad, from 2000 to the end of 2020. This chart was made in the year 2002, although the book was published in 2006. The chart is also 100% true.

Chapter One

122 New Prophecies

- Barack Obama, the President of the U.S., will have two good years in the beginning of his presidency but in the end will be rejected by many of the American people. The storms of the year 2010 and 2011 will become major problems and far worse than hurricanes in 2004 and 2005.

- The United States will have two more black presidents in the very near future. The second may be in the year 2013 or at the latest 2017.

- A father and then his son will be elected president of the U.S. shortly after Barack Obama leaves the White House.

- The U.S will have a problem with AIG around 2011 and possibly 2012. In a very big step to restore the economy back on the road to recovery, the government will totally control AIG for means of national security.

- Hurricanes and other major storms will be a problem in the year 2010 and worse in 2011. This will affect the President's plan to restore the American economy along with other plans to return ethics within the banking and insurance industries.

- The Nation of Islam will consider having a presidential candidate in the race for the White House. But the most powerful leaders of the nation will reject that move. Uncle Sam and Jessie Jackson will be at the forefront of this move. The timing is off. Jessie's last pick will be the one.

- December 21, 2012 will be just another day in the lives of Americans but by January and beyond events will occur that will drastically change the way we live in the world. Days after December 21, 2012 will be the beginning of a New World Order.

- In 2011 there will be a biblical David type person that will come into the American political environment. He will spring from either the grassroots or Congress. There will be changes to the laws of the land and crime as we know it today will end. Many judges will lose their jobs and be replaced by spiritual leaders.

- In 2013 there will be an important person in U.S. politics with the letter A and M in his last name. He will become the second elected black president. However, there may be one other person in office for about two years before he gets there.

- Florida politicians may look back in hindsight and regret the decision to allow State Farm's homeowner's insurer to pull out of Florida after major storms hit the state in 2010 and 2011.

- Jacksonville, Florida will be a major area of refuge for many people in America. This area will escape most of the flooding and other natural disasters that will confront the U.S. in the very near future. Moreover, the economy will not be as bad as in other areas.

- 2009 will be better economically than in 2010 and 2011. 2009 may seem like a bad year but compared to the years to come 2009 is a good one.

- There will be a President in the U.S. who will have a biblical name when the country comes out of the judgment it is in. There will be peace in the nation for a long time when the true royal families rule.

- When trouble hits Obama's camp he will look for a man that is cunning with the media and a savvy player in Washington in order to help relieve the problems that will confront him, problems caused by natural disasters and economic hardship around 2011 and beyond.

- Jesse Jackson will be seen as a major player in the lives of many black politicians that are to be elected to the White House. Indirectly or directly he will be involved.

- Corporations controlled by banking interests will become a more apparent problem in the nation and the lives of Americans. This will be seen as a battle in the Valley much like the biblical days of Saul and David.

- 2013 will experience a depression in America and around the globe. But there will be some areas in the U.S. better off than others.

- In the years 2009, 2010 and 2011 there will be many wise people preparing for December 21, 2012 and subsequent years to come. There will be many Christians who will not see the truth in the words of prophecy. They should understand that the will of the greater Good is to prepare them for the time of hardship. They should have food storage, gold and be in a location for their protection. 2009, '10 and '11 will be called "years of warning".

- The years following 2012 will be a time of tremendous troubles in the U.S. People should look for a person or prophet that has been chosen to lead the nation through difficult times. It is the only way out for the nation!

- Greco-Roman myths taught in the gospel have blinded many in Western Civilization. There are many hidden truths that can guide America away from troubles that it will confront in the coming years. In addition, many people will lose their lives because of their failure to see the Noah type prophet that will come to this nation. Many of them will depend on their preachers over the one the Bible said will come. And they will miss the proverbial boat. The natural disasters that follow will claim a large number of lives. Watch out for the years 2010, '11, '16 and 2017; these will be some of the worst hurricane seasons.

- The year 2013 will bring economic plagues to the nation. The social environment will be out of order. Many corporations will be under attack by the American people, bringing about a war between the corporation and the people. Moral, social and economic stress will bring about many ills in the lives of Americans.

- 2013 will bring about a revolution of change in America. This revolution will not destroy the Corporation that is helping people but will change the way it will be run.

- 2013 will bring about the beginning of fair labor and banking practices. Church and government will begin to think as one as time continues.

- 2014 the economy will be grievously bad in America. And the struggling stock market will have many asking, "what stock market?" War will still be in the Middle East but then will quickly end.

- 2014 many people will not want to leave their homes. The housing market will be worse than ever. People won't have money to pay their loans. These socio-economic problems will cause many laws to be changed in favor of people over the Corporation. And many of these laws will be changed within months.

- 2015 the people will have more control of the nation than ever before. This year will be good but the trouble is not yet over. The years to follow 2016 and 2017 are going to be some of the most trying times in American history. Natural tragedies from the Gulf of Mexico, up through the U.S. will see storms, high winds or even fires, which will seem like brimstone is falling to earth and on the nation. These disasters and large economic losses for America will cause the people of God to open their hearts to the right lifestyle and true government for all people.

- 2017 will be a very grievously bad year for natural disasters. The waters from the hurricanes and other disasters will cause large floods that will turn many cities and towns into swamplands.

- 2018 will open the years of peace in America. The people will begin to push the government into the ideas of the Greater good. These ideas will help all Americans rebuild their lives. The problems that would hinder the races from becoming all that they can be will be removed.

- 2018 the leading families will be in tune with the nation and the needs of the world in general.

- 2020 the church will change in many ways in its beliefs because of more enlightened views by many regarding God and salvation.

- There will be three black men elected President of the U.S. Barack Obama is the first; the second will come from the state of Florida; the third will be the son of the second.

- The ethics committee will have their work cut out for them from 2011 through 2018 in this nation. The people will demand it!

- American churches will lose many in their congregation because of the belief in tithes and offerings. People will begin to understand that these tithes are paid as taxes to the government and that the church is not being truthful. Before 2021 this is going to be a problem for the church.

- In 2050 the Christian cross will not be taught about a human sacrifice, but instead will be taught about the Leonardo Da Vinci code of the Vitruvian Man, "man know thyself", head (moral), feet (economic), right hand (political), left hand (social), heart and stomach area (appetite and diet). The cross philosophy, the five keys or five points of "man know thyself", will be in the new world teaching of Christianity.

- By 2040 most Christians will begin abstaining from meat. Many Christians will begin to see from the eyes of spiritual leaders that the Bible is a history book that tells of the future of America.

- Reptilian humans will be understood by about 20% of the American and European world. Power over the people will come to an end after December 21, 2012. The cataclysm of Venus reptilians underground will be understood by the 20%.

- Saudi Arabia will be in conflict with the United States. Time will eventually reveal the truth that will be hidden from the American people.

- Jacksonville, Callahan and other areas of North Florida will be a new central location of American government. Some will call it the land of Juda, the place of safety. By 2015, '16, '17, a large movement of people will migrate to the area. This area will be seen as the American land of Goshen.

- All races will be left in awe at the events that they will see, many things that have not been told by the leaders of their faith. A time of immense change will occur from 2013 through 2021.

- Barack Obama's morals will hang in the air for the world to see in the last two years of his presidency. A senator or governor will run to his aid. He will eventually be cleared by the next President. It will be like David helping his lord Saul.

- If the new senator or governor of the State of Florida in the year 2010 is black and his last name is Armstrong he will be the next elected President of the U.S. He will be a reincarnated spirit of King David.

- World powers will change. Evil spirits or storms plague the White House in the storm months of 2010 and 2011. Troublesome events overturn many plans to boost the economy. May God Bless America!

- If Obama has two terms his Vice President may be President of the U.S. but for only two years. He will not be able to rule sufficiently. Government looks for a new leader.

- Justice and judgment is the political platform of the next elected President after Obama. Unjust companies will not like some of his policies but America will grow. The economy will be turned around and justice will prevail in the year 2021.

- The nation will build upon the Rock of Salvation through new laws, new beliefs, better people, a new Nation and the light of America.

- Real estate goes up in the southeast area of the U.S.. Many new homes will be needed in 2016 and 2018. It will be as though the West is moving East for safe housing and fewer major storms.

- Laws on marriage will change in 2021. "More than one woman per man," Isaiah 4:1. Sins in church: women with no husbands, men with no wives. Stop the greater evil, God is looking at it all!

- There will be many years of peace and a Golden Age for the world. Small communities helping each other for a better world, God with mankind.

- Space ships become ordinary things, the knowledge of other worlds become common. Secrets are revealed, religion changes but the belief in God is still in place. A new time, new world may occur in 2090, 2100 or many years before, only time will tell.

- Michelle Obama, biblical character, good for the people. She will be known for a long time in history with only good words to say. A world icon. Place no time on her kindness.

- Banking community is at war with Uncle Sam forces. Long battles will occur with large companies in a fight to the end. Government will win. Major Changes in banking by 2018. There will be new rules and new laws.

- The organization (The Rock) will have world wide power. Many people will be a part of this organization. Governments will respect its power which will start in America but will spread to all parts of the world representing a covenant to God, covenant to the people; one nation, one people.

- Jesus is a code name for Lewis the people soon learn. Many French kings had the name; Louis XIV, the Sun King. When the plot is revealed many people will understand the Bible and history much better. The black slave girl is the true blood line.

- The blood line of Jesus will be revealed in America. The secret must not be told before the Roman Catholic Popes have ended. May God Bless America; new world, new Nation.

- Large winds in South Florida. Problems in the Keys, hurricanes in June, July, August. Two years, 2011, 2017. The judgment is here. North Floridians on the Westside beware! God wants changes in His people.

- Former President George W. Bush's brother, Jeb, stepped toward the White House in 2006 then turns back only to step a 2nd time, this time for a senate seat in the House but decided against the pursuit. Twenty years will pass before his next chance but his time is up. Other families are in power; new nation, new times.

- Black migration from all parts of the nation move to the Southeastern states for jobs, temperate weather, religious beliefs, safety, etc. There are many changes in laws and many changes in leadership. Economics and prophecy are all justifications for the move, but not the only reasons.

- The man born across from the gulf will be as a great King, says Nostradamus writing C5Q84. The year 2013 or 2017, the American people will see the man. He will be challenged by the nations of the world but will stand the test. A God sent man, time will tell.

- Many people will overcome the problems in America's economy through careful planning. Some will take the right road, some will take the wrong road, but all will learn. Recession over depression begins in 2011. No denying it by the leaders anymore!

- 2018 the Great God and his Christ will rule the nation of America. True change is in the works. A time when man will begin to help mankind and vice-versa. A blood line of leaders will begin to rule. Some old families will not return.

- A dead people will begin to come alive. Also the lost people will begin to find their way. When December 21, 2012 begins to show its head the mind of the people will change, then their body will begin to be changed.

- "Release the four events that will happen upon the Gulf of Mexico," the angels will say. Louisiana, Mississippi, Alabama, Illinois, will have large bodies of water in many areas where there was land. These events happen in 2016 and 2017.

- Many boats will be needed. The floods will cover a large number of homes. Dead bodies could be avoided by buying small engine boats with aluminum tubes and canvas and having plenty of water. Louisiana and South Florida experience heavy rains and massive flooding in 2016 and 2017 as has not been seen since America became a nation. Men and beasts that are found in the devastated lands and not in the safe areas shall die. May God Bless America!

- The nation's economy will say to its people, "very bad men's hearts must change for the greater good". Many crops are lost, many lives are in shambles. These things could be avoided. The Noah prophet is in the land. North Florida, South Georgia is the land of Goshen.

- 2010 and 2011 will see swamps caused by flooding. The rulers heart need changing; fairness to all people, a judgment in the land. What God will do next, bad or good is your choice. Love toward all people is all that is needed. The worst, storms sent by God is not over. This is "The Judgment".

- 2000 to beyond 2021, Deuteronomy, 18:15, 18, 19, the Lord thy God will raise up unto thee a prophet from the midst of thee, of thy brethren, like unto me unto him ye shall hearken; I will raise them up a prophet from among their brethren, like unto thee, and will put my words in his mouth; and he shall speak unto them all that I shall command him. And it shall come to pass, that whosoever will not hearken unto my words which he shall speak in my name, I will require it of him.

- In the years after 2018 many people will begin to understand that the Holy Bible was written for the U.S. and that the writings of the Bible that mentions the plague of Egypt or events in other nations like Assyria and Ninevah is also about the USA. The whole book is about America and how God will deal with this nation and its people. That is a truth many churchgoers have not understood at this time in history. New world, new teaching, May God be the truth.

- Will there be good times in our future? Truly there will be hundreds of years of peace, a very good time on the earth and in this land we call America. But the judgment must come so the mind of man will change. This is God's plan for mankind. The judgment then we should have over 900 years of peace on the earth.

- Like the weather was a big part of the victory of the revolutionary war in the days of George Washington, so will it be a big part in the turning of this nation from a warring nation to a nation of peace. The years 2004 and 2005 were bad years with hurricanes. So will the years 2010 and 2011, with hurricanes on American soil.

- The judgment will be 21 years in this nation's history. Although many economic forecasters will think the economy will improve soon. Sad to say, it will only get worse. 2011 will be an economic nightmare to many home and business insurance companies.

- 2021 criminal judges will not alone do the job of handling justice. The people will demand change that provides for more fairness for everyone. The judicial system will change due to the general public's demand and of government's new way of thinking how justice should be handled. A new philosophy of the greater good to all mankind will be introduced by a new leader.

- The housing projects in America that breed poverty and crime and have been left behind will be destroyed by the government. The original conception of these projects was designed to be temporary housing but have now forgotten these people. A new order of leadership will help them come out of this environment. For this cause the Greater Good will make America pay. From 2000 to 2021 the agenda is to bring true peace to the nation. The Greater Good will have America pay for their sins through many plagues. May God Bless America? Time must change by 2018.

- The stock market will come to an end. For a period of time people will begin to make different choices in law and the way the system is run and money is loaned. New laws will be created to determine who gets the money and who does not. When it comes to business loans the year 2021 on will bring about many acts of equality.

- The Egyptian Messiah and Jesus will be understood by many young Christians as a person of our day and time. The year 1954 will be significant to his birth rather than 2000 years ago as presently thought. This truth will be one of many things that will change Christianity as we know it today. The blood line of the person we call Jesus will be found in America. Before 2035 many will know this to be true.

- Although many have been conquered by the cross this will change. A new religious philosophy will cover the land. The powers of a God man will be in the land. Many people will see things that have never been seen before now. Many will die because of their disbelief. The natural disasters will work with the God man: Revelation 11:15, "And the seventh angel sound; and there were great voices in heaven, saying the kingdoms of this world are become the kingdoms of our Lord, and of his Christ; and he shall reign for ever and ever". This time is to start around 2018.

- Will America become a monarchy? In the days of George Washington the founding fathers wanted a President that was in opposition to a monarchy. They knew George had no living son that could reign and a child of Washington's born from a slave could not at that time be called to the Presidency. At that time it was not going to happen, but will it in the near future?

- September 2010 and into 2011 AIG will become a big problem for the President of the U.S. The problem will not go away until after AIG falls and a new system is in its place. May God Bless America!

- The land mass will change; the American monarchy. The new leaders will see that it will be the best thing to do to save the nation from outside forces. Before 2028 it will be well on its way.

- Clovis, Louis I and all other of the Louis', like the Sun King; Louis XIV to Louis Philippe, will be revealed. The age of peace, the French Kings by the will of the church is given the coming Jesus' code name. The old Merovingian legend identifies the fleur-de-lys with the French and it should be noted the name Clovis, Lois, Loys and Louis are identified. But the true man that is the fleur-de-lys will be found in the area of the St. Johns

River vicinity in Jacksonville, Florida. The area where the first Frank settlement of the New World was built, a religious colony. This will be understood by many between the years 2021-2028.

- Now Uncle Sam says to America, whom have I oppressed? You see, I give you Barack Obama. Whose ass have I taken and whom have I defrauded? Whose ox have I taken? The election of this President from the government's point of view was to show the world America's fairness and truth in 2009.

- The government of the U.S. would like its people to embrace the tune, We Shall Overcome", in the years 2009 and beyond.

- The thought of the anointed one is what this government wants its people to think of when seeing or hearing President Barack Obama. The media will broadcast that idea into American life for two years, 2009, 2010.

- The tune from the government, let's build a New Nation. Forget the past and look forward to the future. Don't look for reparations. Don't look for benefits that were owed to you in the past. These years are about building our future from this point, 2009-2013.

- The code is found in Psalm 89:13, the year 2013 will call him out; a man of power, a man of justice and judgment will be the next elected President.

- Will there be a king in America in the year 2018 or will there be a President? Time will tell.

- The year 2013 the very rich who are not suffering economically with the personal bills and have greed for more riches prospering for themselves only. Ideas need to change.

- For nine years some American people will be taken from the bottom rung and placed on top and the top rung will move to the bottom; new leadership in America in the area of politics and finance. All types of business ventures will be affected in 2017 and beyond.

- President Barack Obama is loved by many Americans, regardless of color, creed or culture. He has been elected four years to the White House. Many believe that he will have two terms (eight years). The prophecies say that either he will have six years with another person running his office the last two or he will have four years and the second black President will be elected. For eight or 12 years, only time will truly tell.

- If President Barack Obama has a second term he would have to fight against the cooperation in the area of banking and industry. These would be the hardest of America's battles, harder than the Great Depression of the 1930s.

- In the last two years of President Obama's Presidency, the corporations of America will attack him directly and indirectly, morally, socially, politically and economically. They will try to defeat him. God has a ram senator or governor in the bush. He will fight for his cause and they will be defeated.

- These states will see floods; Illinois, East Missouri, West Kentucky, West Tennessee, East Arkansas, Mississippi and Louisiana. Waters from Lake Michigan to the Gulf of Mexico by 2017 will see massive flooded areas. All of America will be affected.

- The years 2010 and 2011 will see swamps and floods in some cities north of New Orleans, Louisiana. Jacksonville, Florida will become the land of Goshen, safe area. The floods will leave but six years later a river will come.

- After 2012 many people, black and white will be divided on their views of America's future. The safe cities will bring many to their doors for safety and protection from the storms.

- The years 2013 and 2014 will have a plague in the farm areas from the unusual weather changes. This will affect the economy and many companies. Heat will come in waves that will affect the flesh or skin of humans and animals.

- The mafia rule will be converted to a patriot rule under a monarchy. The new leader and the families will make it occur. May God Bless America!

- The last six plagues of Egypt will be in America from 2012-2020. But they will only be understood by one that is called by God to see the true meaning of the symbolism. They are not what they seem. Deuteronomy chapter 18, "I will raise them up a Prophet from among their brethren, like unto thee and will put my words in his mouth, and he shall speak unto them all that I shall command him and it shall come to pass.

- The cross will begin to be seen as a philosophy for mankind. It will be taken from the idea of a human sacrifice to the philosophy of "man, know thy self". The secret will be revealed by new leadership. The new monarchy will spread the world over.

- Jesus or Lewis or Louis, the Messiah, will be understood by God's chosen people. The old church has hidden truths for hundreds of years but it will be revealed. May God Bless America!

- Skin disease in the year 2014 and before will effect the lives of many people that do not go underground in various locations. America will be affected. Plants will not have any of the problems that humans and other animals will have.

- The years 2016, and 2017 the rain and flood waters will be very bad and grievous in the land. The type of rain that has not been heard of in this nation since records were kept. Hard days come to the working class people of this nation. Top paying leaders will be affected in 2017. The lower class worker will see the vision of the new black leader that will come. The nation will become new and it will overcome its problems in the years ahead.

- The year 2017, the volcanoes could destroy many people living in the areas of the U.S. if they don't wake up to its power. May God Bless America!

- The area of North Florida and South Georgia in the years 2016 and 2017 will be safe areas from the destruction of this nation. Many of Gods chosen people will go to this area to live through the judgment.

- In the year 2018 the old power of this nation will see the consequences of their bad choices. They will see the need for change in the way the nation has treated lower income people and the dawn of a new nation will rise. Jesus will be walking the earth but only a small number of people will know this.

- The leaders of this nation in the year 2018 need to make good choices. They must not go back to their old ways because the next three years are moving toward the age of peace. The bad choices in leadership have taken away from the true growth of the nation. May God Bless America!

- By 2019 armies of foreign lands will be in this nation to help bring about change. Some people in the local cities don't want true change for the nation. The armies will not fight against the lands of Goshen in America. God will bring change that dishonest leadership is attempting to prevent. The economy will be at its bottom but will improve in the years to come.

17

- By the year 2020 segregation in the church will come to an end. Many will go to the right and others to the left but the people will see the need to come together for the sake of the nation and their families.

- The year 2020 the armies will be driven from the land. The armies will come in many ways. We should see it before the end. Economic warfare is used on the American people. The battle is upon the nation.

- The years 2018, 2019, 2020 there will be economic darkness in many of America's states. Some states in the Southeast will not see this darkness. Many of the chosen people will see light in these dark times.

- After 2020 the nation will change its' political ideas. The year of the last plague upon the nation and the death of the leaders that don't have the interest of the people in their heart. This leadership comes to an end. The chosen of God's people will not feel this death.

- The year 2020 is the year of Passover. This year will begin the ending of the judgment of the nation. The whole nation will see this judgment. God's chosen will overcome. A New World Order is at hand. God's will, not man's will.

- By 2020 the power of the old banking system will be changed. Laws created by new leadership will usurp the old banking laws. The old way of doing business will change as well as the ownership of many businesses. The term, "Pharaoh will lose his nation and a new power will rule", will be a part of America's future.

- The British Empire will no longer have power over America. The throne and the power will be given to a family in this nation. The American people will have a new power and the throne. Church and state will be ruled from the new throne in America. The American people will make it come to pass.

- The chosen people will overcome the throne of England and its powers. The nations of the world will be divided on the matter of helping England. During this time the people of America that have been chosen by God to rule will win the nation and the power of the throne.

- The problem of the hurricanes of 2018 will cause an event in 2020 that will determine who have true power over the nation. Some people in America and England will have no way to hold power over America. The leadership and people uncover the power that has been kept hidden from the nation.

- The Vatican will change its location when a world priest steps to the throne. America will be the new location for the Vatican after earthquakes destroy Rome.

- 2031 The Golden Age has come, no large cities like before. Nations working together as one. Many people wish to see these days.

- God's places a power in motion to destroy the people that have concealed the knowledge of his true royal family. That bloodline will rule in the West. A hidden truth will be revealed. Church folks are lost to the biblical knowledge of Jesus' (Son of Man) royal bloodline who will rule this nation.

- White church mafia revealed, black church mafia revealed. New laws, new teaching. By the end of the year 2010 he will be elected to the U.S. Senate or be the next governor of Florida. He will be born in a former fortress town.

- Carole will be the name of the wife of the next elected President of the USA. Will it be the senator's or the governor's wife? Only God knows.

- The lost city of Atlantis is under the sands. The location is between Florida and the Island of Cuba, north of the Tropic of Cancer and around 80 degrees longitude. North from Tropic of Cancer up to 75 miles radius from longitude 80 degrees esoteric, the Holy Bible and a thought from Edgar Cayce gave a path to the secret of the times. This is a place that an individual must be very careful because the Garden of Eden is hidden in a dimension of time in the area. And if you are not the one to be there, don't go.

- In Psalm 89:13, a mighty Arm:strong is thy one, and high is thy political one. Justice and judgment are the habitation of thy throne, mercy and truth shall go before thy face.

Chapter Two

The Seven Seals of Revelation

Revelation 1:13-19; "Write the things, which thou has seen, (the past) and the thing which are, (the present) and the thing which shall be here after; (future)"

Revelation 5:1 The Seal Book

The book that John saw represented the real history of the world; the past, present and future of mankind. John was given the privilege of seeing what the eyes of God had seen, and also what the recording angel had written. He saw seven great days of this planet's journey with man, from Adam to the days of the Son of Man; seven thousand years, in which our earth will fulfill her mortal mission, laboring with man six days, and resting upon the seventh, a period of sanctification, although these days do not include the period of our earth's creation. They are limited to earth's temporal existence. Time is considered as distinct from eternity. We had four thousand of these years pass before Jesus, and two thousand years has gone by since. Consequently, earth's long week is drawing to a close. This is a time of thought and of solemn meditation. We have opened into the Sabbath of the world.

THE OPENING OF THE FIRST SEAL

The First Seal

"And I saw when the Lamb opened one of the seals, and I heard, as it was the noise of thunder, one of the four beasts saying, 'Come and see.'

"And I saw and beheld a white horse; he that sat on him had a bow; and a crown was given unto him; and he went forth conquering, and to conquer."

Many of these events, as John saw them, pertained to someone on a white horse (the emblem of victory); who had a bow (weapon of war); wore a crown (the garland or wreath of a conqueror); and who went forth conquering and to conquer (that is, was victorious in war)... it is clear that the most transcendent happenings involved Enoch and his ministry. And it is interesting to note that what John saw was not the establishment of Zion and its removal to heavenly spheres, but the unparalleled wars in which Enoch, as a general over the armies of the saints, went forth, conquering and to conquer.

Genesis 5:22; "And Enoch walked with God after he begat Methuselah three hundred years, and begat sons and daughters."

Genesis 5:24 "And Enoch walked with God: and he was not; for God took him."

Truly, never was there a ministry such as Enoch's, and never a conqueror and general who was his equal! How appropriate that he should ride the white horse of victory in John's apocalyptic vision!

THE FIRST SEAL

If you would look closely, we will see the first one thousand years of the planet Earth's temporal existence that is considered as distinct from Eternity...

Now if we look at the genealogy of the First Seal, that is from the time of Adam, years were numbered, until Enoch was taken up, that was 984 years of the First Seal.

If we may look closely at Genesis the fifth, this is the chapter of the generation of Adam. Adam was one hundred and thirty years of age, in temporal existence, and a son named Seth was born unto him.

Seth lived a hundred and five years, and begat Enos. Enos lived ninety years, and begat Cainan. Cainan lived seventy years, and begat Mahalaleel. Mahalaleel lived sixty-five years, and begat Jared. Jared lived one hundred sixty-two years, and he begat Enoch.

Through addition, we can see that, from Adam's days being counted until Enoch's birth, it is six hundred and twenty-four years. Now if we look at all the days of Enoch's life, which are three hundred sixty, we can see 984 years of Mother Earth's temporal existence, which is 984 years of the First Seal.

These years are between 4000 B.C. to 3000 B.C.

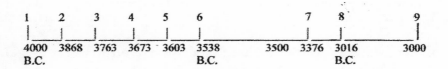

1	2	3	4	5	6	7	8	9
4000 B.C.	3868	3763	3673	3603	3538 B.C.	3500	3376	3016 B.C.	3000

(1)   Adam days were numbered
(2)   Seth's birth
(3)   Enos's birth
(4)   Cainan's birth
(5)   Mahalaleel's birth
(6)   Jared's birth
(7)   Enoch birth
(8)   Enoch was taken up
(9)   The first Seal Ends

The Second Seal

THE SECOND SEAL
THE OPENING OF THE SECOND SEAL

"And when he had opened the Second Seal, I heard the second beast say, 'Come and see.' And there went out another horse that was red: and power was given to him that sat thereon to take peace from the earth, and there was given unto him a great sword."

What is the interpretation of the opening of the Second Seal? Perhaps it was the devil himself, for surely that was the great day of his power, a day of such gross wickedness that every living soul (save eight only) were found worthy of death by drowning, which wickedness caused the Lord God of Heaven to bring a flood upon them. Or if it was not Lucifer, perhaps it was a man of blood, or a person representing many murdering warriors, of whom we have no record. Suffice it to say, that the era from 3000 B.C. to 2000 B.C. was one of war and destruction, these being the favorite weapons of Satan for creating those social, moral, economic, and political conditions in which men lose their souls. Of the wickedness and abominations of Noah's day, the revealed word says:

"And God saw that the wickedness of men had become great in the earth; and every man was lifted up in the imagination of the thoughts of his heart, being only evil continually. The earth was corrupt before God, and it was filled with violence. And God looked upon the earth, and, behold, it was corrupt, for all flesh corrupted it's way upon the earth."

THE SECOND SEAL

In the second seal, we can also see the genealogy of it. Enoch was sixty-five years of age when he begat Noah's grandfather. Noah's grandfather was 187 years old when he begat Noah's father. And Noah's father was 182 years old when he begat Noah. And Noah lived nine hundred and fifty years and died. From knowing the year Enoch was born and the age he was at Methuselah's birth, we can know Methuselah was born 3311 B.C. Lamech was born 3124 B.C., and Noah was born 2942 B.C. Note also that the flood was in the six hundred years of Noah's life, which was 2342 B.C., and he died 1992 B.C. Noah died eight years into the Third Seal, but all of his work was in the Second Seal.

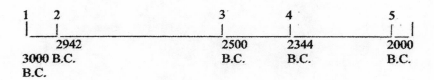

(1) The Second Seal began
(2) Noah's birth
(3) The flood came
(4) Noah's work ended
(5) The Second Seal ended

The Third Seal

THE THIRD SEAL

What is the interpretation of the opening of the Third Seal?

"And when he had opened the Third Seal, I heard the third beast say, 'Come and see.' And I beheld; and lo a black horse; and he that sat on him had a pair of balance in his hand. And I heard a voice in the midst of the four beasts say, 'A measure of wheat for a penny, and three measures of barley for a penny; and see thou hurt not the oil and the wine.'"

As famine follows the sword, so the pangs of hunger gnawed in the bellies of the Lord's people during the Third Seal. From 2000 B.C. to 1000 B.C. as never in any other age of the earth's history, the black horse of hunger influenced the whole history of God's dealings with his people.

The days of Abraham would be the first time the word "famine" was used in the scriptures of the Holy Bible. God, the Almighty, had Abraham leave his fatherland of Ur and take Sarah, his wife; Lot, his brother's son, and all his substance; and other souls who were with him, and go into the land of Canaan. Abraham struggled to gain sufficient food to keep alive.

This search for sustenance was yet burdening the Lord's people in the days of Jacob, who sent his sons to Egypt to buy corn from the granaries of Joseph, his son. In that day, famine was over all the face of the earth, and it was only through divine intervention that Jacob and the beginning members of the house of Israel were saved from the fate of Haran (Genesis 41:53-57;42; and 44) And in the days of their sojourn in the wilderness, the millions of Jacob's seed who followed Moses out of Egyptian bondage, lest they perish for want of bread, were fed for forty years with manna from heaven (Exodus 16). Truly, the third seal was a millennium in which hunger among men affected the whole course of God's dealings with his people.

REVELATION 6:6

"A measure of wheat for a penny." This strange accounting of the price of wheat and barley seems baffling to us today, but knowledge of the monetary units and customs of John's time helps us to better understand what the voice declared. John's readers would have clearly understood it. A measure (Greek choenix) was the usual amount of a day's allowance or ration. The penny (denarius) was a small silver coin of Roman mintage – although it is hard to determine the equivalent value in today's inflated economy, it is known that a denarius was the typical wage for a day's work in those times. Thus, to spend one day's wages to buy only enough food for one person for one day clearly points out that these were famine prices. Three measures of barley could be purchased for a penny, but barley was a much inferior grain for human consumption, and was generally used only in times of great hunger. The fact that the rider had balances in his hand suggests that the scarcity of food was such that it had to be doled out with exactness. "Hurt not the oil and the wine" meant that enough food should be preserved so that man would not utterly perish in the famine conditions of that time.

THE THIRD SEAL

If we will look at the generation of Shem until Abram, whose name was changed to Abraham, we will note that Abraham was born 2045 B.C. To get this year of his birth, remember the year of Shem's birth.

In the year 1970 B.C., Abraham, his wife, and Lot departed out of Haran. During this time, the 1900s B.C., the bible first tells of famines, in the twentieth chapter – Genesis, tenth verse.

Abraham lived one hundred and seventy-five years before he died. His death was in the year 1870 B.C. In the year 1945 B.C., Isaac was born. At the age of thirty, his sons, Esau and Jacob, were born of Isaac in the year 1885 B.C. Genesis 26:1 tells of famine in the land at this time of history.

Note, at this time also, that Esau despised his birthright.

Genesis 25:33-34 the birthright included a double portion of the inheritance (Deuteronomy 21:15-17) and the privilege of the priesthood. Jacob was ninety years of age in the year 1795 B.C., when he begat Joseph. Joseph was the Hebrew boy who was sold into Egypt by his brothers and became the great prime minister of the pharaoh.

The story of Joseph is one of the most interesting dramas of all time. Pharaoh was so pleased with Joseph's wisdom that he chose him to oversee the grain storing of all Egypt. For seven years, there were abundant crops. Then came the famine, or bad years, between the good years. No grain had been saved in Canaan. Joseph died in the year 1685 B.C., being one hundred ten years old.

In the 1600s B.C., Joseph died, as did all his brethren and all of that generation. The children of Israel were fruitful, increased abundantly, multiplied, were exceeding mighty, and the land was filled with them. Moses was born in 1623 B.C.; the children of Israel came to the land of Canaan in 1503 B.C.; and in 1503 B.C., Joshua was the ruler. David ruled seven and a half years before the year 1000 B.C.

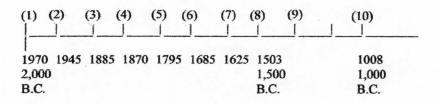

(1)	(2)	(3)	(4)	(5)	(6)	(7)	(8)	(9)		(10)
1970	1945	1885	1870	1795	1685	1625	1503			1008
2,000							1,500			1,000
B.C.							B.C.			B.C.

(1)   The Third Seal began
(2)   Abraham, his wife, and Lot depart out of Haran
(3)   Isaac's birth
(4)   Esau's and Jacob birth
(5)   Abraham died
(6)   Joseph's birth
(7)   Joseph's death (8) Moses birth
(9)   Children of Israel came to the land of Canaan and Joshua ruled
(10) David is King
(11) The Third Seal ends

The Fourth Seal

THE OPENING OF THE FOURTH SEAL

"And when he had opened the Fourth Seal, I heard the noise of the fourth beast say, 'Come and see.'"

"And I looked and beheld a pale horse: and his name that sat on him was Death, and Hell followed with him. And power was given unto them over the fourth part of the earth, to kill with sword, and with hunger, and with death, and with the beasts of the earth..."

During the Fourth Seal, from 1000 B.C. to the coming of our Lord, death rode roughshod through the nations of men, and hell was at his heels. Thus, the slain among the ungodly in this age of bloodshed whether by sword, by famine, by pestilence, or by wild beast were, at their death, cast down to hell. This is the millennium of those great kingdoms and nations whose wars and treacheries tormented and overran again and again the people Jehovah had chosen to bear his name. This is also the general era in which the Lord's own people sent countless numbers of their own brethren to untimely graves.

THE FOURTH SEAL

This Fourth Seal started with God's own people that he had chosen turning to the heathen ways. Human sacrifices were forbidden in the law of Moses (Leviticus 18:21;20:2-5; Deuteronomy 18:10). An example of this is given in II Kings 3:27, when during a siege, Mesha, King of Moab, sacrificed his eldest son and heir apparent to the throne upon the city wall as a burnt offering. Israel and her allies withdrew in horror.

Some of the Israelites adopted the practice of sacrificing sons and daughters. Both Ahaz (II Kings 16:3; II Chronicles 28:1-3) and Manasseh (II Kings 21:6; II Chronicles 33:6) fell into this heathen custom and "made their sons to pass through the fire" – a term used to express the horror of human sacrifice (*Wycliffe Bible Dictionary* Charles F. Pfeiffer, Howard F. Vos, John Rca Editors).

II Kings 17:17-23; "And they caused their sons and their daughters to pass through the fire, and used divination and enchantments, and sold themselves to do evil in the sight of the Lord, to provoke him to anger.

Therefore, the Lord was very angry with Israel, and removed them out of his sight: there was none left but the tribe of Judah only. Also Judah kept not the commandments of the Lord their God, but walked in the statutes of Israel which they made.

"And the Lord rejected all the seed of Israel and afflicted them, and delivered them into the hand of spoilers, until he had cast them out of his sight.

"For he rent Israel from the house of David and they made Jeroboam the son of Nebat King: and Jeroboam drove Israel from following the Lord, and made them sin a great sin.

"For the children of Israel walked in all the sins of Jeroboam which he did; they departed not from them;

"Until the Lord removed Israel out of his sight, as he had said by all his servants the prophets. So was Israel carried away out of their own land to Assyria unto this day."

As Assyria became the nation to rule over the people of God and others, it became a war-loving nation. (Isaiah. 33:19). Its people were much more aggressive than their neighboring Semitic cohorts of Babylonia. This nation had a spirit of competition to kill and destroy. The nation of Assyria had many deities. Assyria was the nation that the prophet Jonah cried unto in the great city Nineveh. Jonah cried against it because their wickedness had come up before the Lord God. About 612-609 B.C., the Assyrian Empire gave way to the Neo-Babylonian Empire led by Nabopolassar and his son, Nebuchadnezzar II. After the fall of Nineveh to the Babylonians and Medes in 612 B.C., Haran and Carchemish soon surrendered, and the lion of Assyria gave way to the eagle of Babylon. Babylonia became significant in world history during the Chaldean Empire of Nebuchadnezzar (sixth century B.C.). Babylon became the terror of Western Asia. This Empire of Babylon besieged the King of Judah (Daniel 1:1-5). One of the children was the prophet Daniel, who became a powerful man in the kingdom. This prophet foresaw that the nations of the world would rise and fall until the end, when God the Almighty would seat a kingdom that would rule for many years to come. He also was the prophet that was put into the lion's den to be killed by the animals but survived.

As time continued, the Empire of Babylon gave way to Cyrus, King of Persia. These Persians moved across the Iranian plateau and occupied the region of the Persian Gulf to the Great Salt Desert. Cyrus's mother was a Median wife daughter of the Median King Astyages. Cyrus, in war, revolted against Medes and all that Medes controlled fell to Cyrus the Great. During these thousand years, death and hell would began their ride into three millenniums. Cyrus also was able to take Babylon without a siege, and marched into the city as a deliverer in 539 B.C.

As time continued in this millennium, in about the fourth century B.C., Philip II and his son, Alexander the Great, made a conscious effort to bring Greek culture to their kingdom. Philip built the military capability of Macedon. He passed this army to his son, Alexander the Great. This army was excellent in launching the Panhellenic wars. Alexander was fighting war after war in his quest to control a large area of territory, but as time continued King Pyrrhus of Epirus led an army to Italy to help the Greeks in the southern part of the peninsula take a stand against Rome and unify Italy. Roman warfare in Greece lasted fifty years, with the Roman annexation of Greece and the creation of the Macedonian and Achaean provinces.

The Roman Empire was the last empire to rule under the power of these thousand years. The city of Rome became a place that was to dominate the Italian peninsula and Italy. The Roman Empire dominated the Mediterranean world. These Italic tribes intermarried with the Indo-European stock along the Mediterranean. Rome wrestled over control with the Etruscans, and war began in that area. By the year 265 B.C., the Romans had taken control of the entire peninsula. Rome united the peninsula when she became involved in a series of wars, the Punic Wars, with the Carthaginians. Rome built a large navy at Carthage (264-241 B.C.). Then Rome turned its attention to the Eastern Mediterranean. During this time, 146 B.C., Rome had annexed all of Greece. Some of the Roman rulers were Marius, Sulla, Pompey, Julius Caesar, Crassus, Mark Antony, and others. During the Fourth Seal, from 1000 B.C. to the coming of Jesus, death rode through these nations of men and hell was at his heel. This was truly an age of bloodshed. This pale horse also will carry his powers into the next millennium. Although Jesus was born at the very end of the thousand years, His teachings of a political power would all point to the future years of the time of the Son of Man. This millennium also produced more prophets of God than ever before.

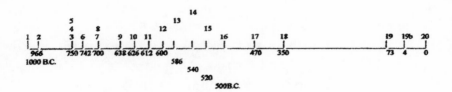

(1)   The Fourth Seal began

(2)   Solomon is king; began building the temple

(3)   Hosea came on the scene

(4)   Hosea was a prophet in the Kingdom of Israel

(5)   Amos, Hebrew prophet

(6)   Isaiah began his prophecies

(7)   Jonah, a Hebrew prophet

(8)   Micah, Judean prophet

(9)   Zephaniah, a prophet in Judah

(10)   Jeremiah, Hebrew prophet

(11)   Nahum, Hebrew prophet

(12) Daniel, well-known Biblical prophet
(13) Ezekiel, Jewish prophet
(14) Obadiah, Servant of the Lord
(15) Haggi, a Jewish prophet
(16) Zechariah, a prophet in Jerusalem
(17) Malachi, name given to a prophet in Jerusalem
(18) Joel, prophesied in Judah
(19) Herod-Great, ruled all Palestine
(19b) Herod-Great died
(20) This is supposed to have been the time of Jesus's birth and the end of the Fourth Seal

THE FIFTH SEAL

The Fifth Seal

What is the interpretation of the Opening of the Fifth Seal?

"And when he had opened the Fifth Seal, I saw under the altar the souls of them that were slain for the word of God, and for the testimony which they held: And they cried with a loud voice, saying, 'How long, O Lord, Holy and true, dost thou not judge and avenge our blood on them that dwell on the earth?' And white robes were given unto every one of them; and it was said unto them, that they should rest yet for a little season, until their fellow servants also and their brethren that should be killed as they were should be fulfilled."

Our Lord's work and ministry are everywhere, taught in holy writ; the facts relative to the post-meridian apostasy and the perversion of the saving truths and powers are also abundantly taught in other sacred writings. And so, what is more natural than to find the Lord revealing here that portion of the sealed book which deals with the doctrine of martyrdom, which was an ever-present possibility, one that completely occupied their thoughts and feelings? They knew that, to forsake all to follow Jesus, they might, if fate so decreed, be called to lay down their lives for Him, who had given all of His adult life for their growth of self-empowerment. In an almost death-inviting sense, the meridian of time was the dispensation of martyrdom.

When looking at the writing of this Fifth Seal, it doesn't only tell you of the years from 0 to 1000 A.D., but also a little about the next two millenniums. Look closely: "I saw under the altar the souls of them that were slain for the word of God." This shows males and females being able to come before God the Almighty, without a high priest on earth between them and God. But this practice will cost some to be slain. Augustus was the architect of the Pax Romana, or Roman Peace. When Jesus came on the scene, the law of Augustus made the old religious rituals again a part of the affairs of state. In time, worship of the emperor began. All people within the empire had to obey. This Roman worship was in opposition to the teaching of Jesus. The saints that followed Jesus believed in One God and the cross philosophy, "Man, Know Thyself." Jesus' movement, and other religious teachings that were not in line with the Roman ideals were wrong and must be destroyed. The saints became part of the religious martyrdom. The Romans would not, at that time, continue to accept Christianity if they could not see some of their religious beliefs inside of it. There, the human sacrifice in the teachings of Jesus Christianity began, even though the teaching of Moses and others (Leviticus 18:21;20:2-5; Deuteronomy 18:10; II Kings 17:17) were against this type of practice. Even today, this belief in the crucifixion as a sacrifice is the root of Christianity. The Jewish beliefs have always been at odds with this teaching. Many people were killed because they wanted religious freedom. Constantine and others enforced even more despotic control over their subjects. Roman law, history has said, held the people of the empire together with their old beliefs. The writing of the Fifth Seal, **"How long, O Lord, holy and true, dost thou not judge and avenge our blood on them that dwell on the earth?"** points to the time of the martyrdom to be long, but how long? This terror will go into the next thousand years as well. The saints are asking how long until the judgment.

The response is in the next line: **"And white robes were given unto every one of them and it was said unto them, that they should rest yet for a little season, until their fellow servants also and their brethren, that should be killed as they were, should be fulfilled."** This verse is very important to understand. It is pointing out the torment of their fellow servants (the ones of their millennium who will be martyrs of the faith) **"and their brethren,"** showing the ones that are to come after the millennium of the Lord Jesus. But in this Fifth Seal, we can see the age of grace and apostleship (Roman 1:5-6). Although the Holy Bible shows the teachings of Jesus, the Holy Bible also shows his way of seeing things of prophecy. About 99.9 percent of the Christian world has seen the scripture from darkness. Only grace and mercy have saved their souls, not work.

Roman 11:25-27; "For I would not, brethren, that ye should be ignorant of this mystery, lest ye should be wise in your own conceits; that blindness in part is happened to Israel, until the fullness of the gentiles become in.

"And so all Israel shall be saved: as it is written, there shall come out of Sion the Deliverer, and shall turn away ungodliness from Jacob:

"For this is my covenant unto them, when I shall take away their sins."

THE FIFTH SEAL

This seal starts with Jesus and his teaching of the cross philosophy. We must note that the philosophy had been changed by Roman priests and others as Romans came into Christianity. Even many people who were not Christians believed that he was a great and wise teacher. Jesus has probably influenced humanity more than anyone else who ever lived. The teaching of Jesus united people from many lands into a great religious movement that is now the most widespread in the world. Mohammed, the founder of Islam, regarded Jesus as a great prophet and adopted many of his ideas. Democratic beliefs in equality, responsibility, and care for the weak owe much to Jesus' teaching. Although we see Jesus' teaching as a great theology, the government of Rome saw it as a threat. After the age of the apostles, there came a great falling away. The nations of Christians killed many souls because of their religious beliefs. The church itself caused many of these deaths. The church from the Fifth through the Sixth Seal will be at the forefront of martyrdom.

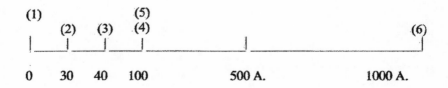

(1)   The Fifth Seal began, as well as what was supposed to have been Jesus birth

(2)   Jesus work began

(3)   Herod Antipas rule ended - he was the king that beheaded John the Baptist and opposed Jesus

(4)   Herod Antipas I rule ended - He was the king that killed the Apostle James, and also many Jews were killed doing his rule

(5)   The Great Falling Away

(6)   The Fifth Seal ends

THE SIXTH SEAL

The Sixth Seal

THE OPENING OF THE SIXTH SEAL

And I beheld when he had opened the Sixth Seal, and, lo, there was a great earthquake; and the sun became black as sackcloth of hair, and the moon became as blood.

"And the stars of Heaven fell unto the earth even as a fig tree casteth her untimely figs when she is shaken of a mighty wind. And Heaven departed as a scroll when it is rolled together; and every mountain and island were moved out of their places. And the kings of the earth, and the great men and the rich men and the chief captains and the mighty men and every bondman, and every free Man, hid themselves in the dens and in the rocks of the mountains; and said to the mountains and rocks, 'Fall on, and hide us from the face of him that sitteth on the throne, and from the wrath of the Lamb: For the great day of his wrath is come; and who shall be able to stand?'"

Chapter seven is a part of the next seal. The seventh chapter of Revelation sums up the years beginning about 2,000 A.D. to the end of the seventh millennium and beyond.

The great earthquake in this Sixth Seal of John's writing from 1000 A.D. to 2000 A.D., shows us of a great movement of people from one continent to the other. This was the start of the Transatlantic slave trade. This event was a part of time when human matter was shifted from one place to the other.

"The sun became black as sackcloth of hair and the moon became as blood." When using this saying as a science project, it will be shown as hard-to-see light, or hard days and the reflection on the moon as hard night. The phrase **"black as sackcloth of hair"** is about farm production. What does all this mean? It means that these activities will take place in the life of the people that God is to choose as a people unto Him . This time between 1000 A.D. to 2000 A.D. not only brought in the transatlantic slave trade, but also the Industrial Revolution. This Industrial Revolution changed society much more than the French Revolution and the Intellectual

Movement of Enlightenment. In the long run, the steam engine, the factory, the railroad, and slave labor changed society. The new technology led to greater wealth (Daniel 12:4). Even Daniel saw this technology would help man **"run to and fro, and knowledge shall be increased."**

"And the stars of heaven fell unto the earth, even as a fig tree casteth her untimely figs, when she is shaken of a mighty wind."

This area points to Israel as a nation in its beginning years, as being the fig tree, untimely figs, and being shaken of a mighty wind. Although Israel became a nation, there were wars and troubles from its beginning. This power that came from the Fourth Seal was still present in the underlining of this Sixth Seal. **"The stars of heaven fell unto the earth."** Men like Martin Luther King Jr., and other great men of history were killed in this Seal. This star and others wanted to change mankind to achieve a greater level of life, but were taken down. We can go through the history of this sixth millennium and see many more stars or great men of history.

When we read the next area of this seal we can see Amos teaching in 8:11-13: **"And the heaven departed as a scroll when it is rolled together; and every mountain and island were moved out of their places."** As new scientific discoveries led to invention, medical research helped people live longer, biology changed ideas, psychology became a science, then many people, even church people, felt they could accept both Darwinism and Christianity.

Amos 8:11-13; "'Behold the days come,' saith the Lord God, 'that I will send a famine in the land, not a famine of bread, nor a thirst for water, but of hearing the words of the Lord:

"And they shall wander from sea to sea, and from the north even to the east, they shall run to and fro to seek the word of the Lord, and shall not find it."

This Sixth Seal goes on to show the event that will continue, even to the year 2000 A.D.

"And the Kings of the earth, and the great men, and the rich men, and the chief captains, and the mighty men, and every bondsman, and every free man, hid themselves in the dens and in the rocks of the mountains; and said to the mountains and rocks, 'Fall on us, and hide us from the face of him that sitteth on the throne, and from the wrath of the Lamb: for the great day of his wrath is come; and who shall be able to stand?'"

This area of scripture is showing the reader how the people of the Christian world were looked at by the eyes of God and the recording angels. The kings, great men, rich men, and others would use the temple and churches to hide their evil. The rich and top men were always tied to the religions of the day. From the slave trade of the Sixth Seal to the end of that seal, there were many evils. The Industrial Revolution had seven deadly sins: unhealthy dangerous factories; impossibly long working hours; child labor; unjust use of women; low wages; slums; and repeated loss of jobs. And the religious leaders many times said nothing about the owners' wrongdoings. Even the people these things were happening to said very little. Industrialization was not the blame for all the social problems of the nineteenth and twentieth centuries. The teaching of the word of God had not been taught totally correct.

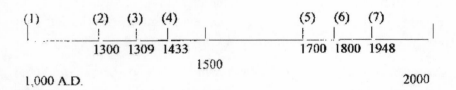

(1) The Sixth Seal began
(2) The Renaissance began in Italy
(3) Martin Luther and the Reformation
(4) The transatlantic slave trade
(5) Age of Invention
(6) Industrial Revolution
(7) Israel became an established nation

THE SEVENTH SEAL

The Seventh Seal

THE OPENING OF THE SEVENTH SEAL

The Seventh Seal is from the years 2000 A.D. to 3000 A.D. Mankind should pay close attention to this seal. This seal's writing is in chapter 8, 9, 10 and 11, but 10 should be looked at separately.

Revelation 8:1; "And when he had opened the Seventh Seal, there was silence in heaven about the space of half and hour."

This verse is opening this seal up to show you that there will be twenty-one years to see God do a great work. In heaven, a day is a thousand years of our time. In doing the math, one thousand divided means one half-hour equals twenty and a half, or twenty-one years.

The events of the trumpets that are to sound in this seal should last a total of twenty-one years, with each trumpet sounding three years.

Revelation 8:2-6; "And I saw the seven angels which stood before God; and to them were given seven trumpets.

"And another angel came and stood at the altar, having a golden censer; and there was given unto him much incense, that he should offer it with the prayers of the saints upon the golden altar which was before the throne.

"And the smoke of the incense, which came with the prayers of the saints, ascended up before God out of the angel's hand.

"And the angel took the censer, and filled it with fire of the altar, and cast it into the earth: and there were voices, and thundering, and lightning , and an earthquake.

"And the seven angels which had the seven trumpets prepared themselves to sound.

These verses are telling the entire world that, in these years, all hell will break loose on earth. This is an age that time must be cut short, or no flesh will be saved. We must understand that these twenty-one years from 2000 to 2021 are of war and natural disaster. In this seal, in the beginning years, people in the area called the earth (America) will move to other locations to survive (earthquake), the wars and natural disaster that are to confront this nation. Please hear this seal because this is the time of the survival of this nation and the world itself. The last four trumpet sounds will be the most devastating time. In the twenty-one years of this seal, the Son of Man will do his teachings, but some people will not know that it will be Him, because they have been taught a false teaching about the way He would appear.

Revelation 8:7; "The first angel sounded, and there followed hail and fire, mingled with blood, and they were cast upon the earth: and the third part of trees was burnt up, and all green grass was burnt up."

This first angel and his trumpet started from the beginning of the year 2000 to the end of 2002; three years. But we must also remember the effect of the trumpet throughout the years to come. Now what is this first angel and trumpet saying? **"And there followed hail and fire mingled with blood, and they were cast upon the earth:"**

This place that these events are to start is called the earth (America). God is at the forefront of these events. Following hail is about economic troubles, because when hail falls, it destroys crops and property. Truly these are the years in this millennium that the American dollar began to fall worldwide. Even in Canada, it fell from $1.34 to $1.18 in just four years, and in other areas of the world, it is much greater.

"Fire mingled with blood"

These first three years of the new millennium also showed war, or the act of war, in our own nation. The 9/11 event on America soil was an act of war against Americans on American soil. This event caused the U.S. to start a war in the land of Iraq. This event is also bringing in St Luke 11:29-36. The verses in Luke 11 also point to Bush as part of the leadership in the conflict.

"And the third part of the trees was burnt up, and all green grass was burnt up."

In this verse, John saw the world divided in thirds: from Adam to Melchizedek was one third; Melchizedek to Jesus was one third; and Jesus to the year 2000 A.D. is one-third. So the third part would be from Jesus time to 2000 A.D. This writing is saying that this third part of man's righteousness must be destroyed, because a great evil has come into it. Part of that evil is the way the Bible is taught. From this teaching, our society went off the path of truth, far from the way God wanted it to be, so a change in the way mankind thinks about right and wrong has to come.

Revelation 8:8-9; "And the second angel sounded, and as it were a great mountain burning with fire was cast into the sea: and the third part of the sea became blood; And the third part of the creatures which were in the sea, and had life, died; and the third part of the ships were destroyed."

These two verses are pointing at the church and the moral view of the American and European people who have the power to change the action of the society. The actions of the morality of the mountain (church) from the end of 2002 to the beginning of 2006 would be tested. And in these years in America, the so-called Christian nation, a homosexual priest was elected to office. Many lesbians and gays came out in behalf of their so-called right to marry the same sex. Morals and church affairs were also a part of the last presidential election that happened at this same time. This trumpet will cause the power that supports bad moral ideals which came from the last millennium to be destroyed.

Revelation 8:10-11; "And the third angels sounded, and there fell a great star from heaven burning as it were a lamp, and it fell upon the third part of the rivers, and upon the fountains of waters; And the name of the star is called wormwood: and the third part of the waters became wormwood; and many men died of the waters, because they were made bitter."

This trumpet is from the beginning of the year 2006 to the end of 2008. This is part of our future from this year of 2006. This trumpet is about now, 2006 to 2008. What is this trumpet saying to us now? It is saying that this is a time for the new philosophy to be taught of the word of God. The great star is about a teacher or teaching that will begin in these years, from 2006 to the end of 2008. The philosophy is a move from God that is found in Jonah 4:6-8.

This person or idea was born at the very end of the last millennium (it **"fell upon the third part of the rivers, and upon the fountains or waters;"**), so this person or idea had to come from among the old teachings or ideas into the true teaching or way of seeing truth . This star is called Wormwood; the word "worm" indicates a movement that will take place. This movement will be connected with the "wood" or "gourd" (the gospel that is not in its fullness). The gourd was a vine plant with a bitter fruit that looked like an orange. This gospel that came from the last two thousand years is what has made the waters bitter. Because the water was made bitter, they did not become bitter when the star fell. Because they were made bitter, this shows they were created bitter. The teaching of this book is a part of the star's movement.

Revelation 8:12-13; "And the fourth angel sounded, and the third part of the sun was smitten, and the third part of the moon and the third part of the stars; so as the third part of them was darkened, and the day shone, not for a third part of it, and the night likewise. And I beheld, and heard an angel flying through the midst of heaven, saying with a loud voice, 'Woe, woe, woe to the inhabitants of the earth by reason of the other voices of the trumpet of the three angels which are yet to sound!'"

These are the years from 2009 to the end of 2011. This trumpet will begin to open the eyes of the elect of God. It will show them that the last two thousand years they have been spiritually dead, and that through grace were they saved, and not by the teaching that they had received. That the Greco-Roman myths teaching in the gospel have blinded the nations of many truths. This trumpet will also begin to open their eyes to the next three trumpets of events. They will understand that God is sending very bad times ahead.

Revelation 9:1-12; "And the fifth angel sounded, and I saw a star fall from heaven unto the earth: and to him was given the key of the bottomless pit. And he opened the bottomless pit; and there arose a smoke out of the pit, as the smoke of a great furnace; and the sun and the air were darkened by reason of the smoke of the pit. And there came out of the smoke locusts upon the earth: and unto them was given power, as the scorpions of the earth have power. And it was commanded them that they should not hurt the grass of the earth, neither any green thing; neither any tree; but only those men which have not the seal of God in their foreheads. And to them it was given that they should not kill them, but that they should be tormented five months: and their torment was as the torment of a scorpion when he striketh a man. And in those days shall men seek death and shall not find it; and shall desire to die, and death shall flee from them. And the shapes of the locusts were like unto horses prepared unto battle and on their heads were as it were crowns like gold, and their faces were as the faces of men. And they had hair as the hair of women, and their teeth were as the teeth of lions. And they had breast plates as it were breast plates of iron, and the sound of their wings was as the sound of chariots of many horses running to battle. And they had tails like unto scorpions and there were stings in their tails; and their power was to hurt men five months. And they had a king over them which is the angel of the bottomless pit whose name in the Hebrew tongue hath his name Abaddon, but in the Greek tongue both his name Apollyon. One woe is past; and, behold, there come two woes more hereafter.

The trumpet of the fifth angel is sounding the time of the first woe. These years, from 2012 to the end of 2014, will be a new awakening for the people of God morally, socially, economically, politically, and in the way they eat and bring ideas and other things in their life. The movement and ideas will come from the third trumpet. It will build leading men that will exercise their power and come against the leaders who are not leading America and the world in the direction God has chosen it to go. This revolution will end the world of the past. This revolution will not destroy the economy, it will change the way it will be run. Fair labor practices, banking practices, church, and government will begin to think as one. Although this trumpet will bring in these ideas, they will reach their highest around 2018-2021. The scorpions are a part of the movement that is in Jonah 4:7-8. This event, along with natural disasters (vehement east wind) and war in the Middle East will change America from the evils that God and the recording angels saw.

Revelation 9:13-21; And the sixth angel sounded, and I heard a voice from the four horns of the golden altar which is before God, saying to the sixth angel which had the trumpet, 'Loose the four angels which are bound in the great river Euphrates.'

"And the four angels were loosed, which were prepared for an hour, and a day, and a month, and a year, for to slay the third part of men.

"And the numbers of the army of the horsemen were two hundred thousand thousand: and I heard the number of them.

"And thus I saw the horses in the vision and them that sat on them, having breastplates of fire, and of jacinth, and brimstone: and the heads of the horses were as the heads of lions; and out of their mouths issued fire and smoke and brimstone.

"By these three was the third part of men killed, by the fire, and by the smoke, and by the brimstone, which issued out of their mouths.

"For their power is in their mouth, and in their tails: for their tails were like unto serpents, and had heads, and with them they do hurt.

"And the rest of the men which were not killed by these plagues yet repented not of the works of their hands, that they should not worship devils, and idols of gold, and silver, and brass, and stone, and of wood: which neither can see, nor hear, nor walk: neither repented they of their murders, nor of their sorceries, nor of their fornication, nor of their thefts.

This Sixth Trumpet is the worst of the worst. This is a time that Americans and the world would think God himself has forsaken it. This time is from the beginning of 2015 to the year 2018. God will shake the world in seeing his presence. It will be a time of natural disaster as never before. America will see natural tragedies from the Gulf of Mexico, up through the nation of America. The storm, whether by rain, by wind, or by fire, will seem as though brimstone was falling to the earth on the nation. These disasters and large economic losses for America will cause the people of God to open their heart to the right lifestyle and true government for the people of the nation.

"Loose the four angels which are bound in the great river Euphrates." This writing is about an area in this nation, as of the Euphrates in the area of Assyria. Looking closely at a map of Assyria in the days of Jonah, the Euphrates looks like, and is in an area like the west coast of Florida. The trumpet shows how the Gulf of Mexico will play a large part in the worst natural disasters in the history of America as a nation. The area of Louisiana, Mississippi, Alabama, Illinois, and other areas could see the hands of God's wrath on their states. But why is this to happen to this nation, the one that said it believes "In God we trust"? The key is to understand where life comes from as concerning a nation. The government is the producer of life, and when that government fails to protect in the way of God, God will cause that nation to fall. Although the trumpets tell of many things that are to happen, we will cover that more in other writings.

THE SEVENTH ANGEL SOUNDED

This is a time all of the people of God want to see. The years from 2018 to 2021 and beyond. The nations of the world will be in an awakened state; a time to truly focus, no more wars, no more bad government, racism, poverty, and other ways mankind is off base with God, the Almighty.

Revelation; "And the seventh angel sounded; and there were great voices in heaven, saying, 'The kingdoms of this world are become the kingdoms of our Lord and of his Christ; and he shall reign for ever and ever.'

"And the four and twenty elders, which sat before God on their seats, fell upon their faces, and worshipped God, saying, 'We give thee thanks, O Lord God Almighty, which art, and worst, and art to come; because thou host taken to thee thy great power, and host reigned.'

"And the nations were angry, and thy wrath is come, and the time of the dead, that they should be judged, and that thou shouldest give, reward unto thy servants the prophets, and to the saints, and them that fear thy name, small and great; and shouldest destroy them which destroy the earth.

"And the temple of God was opened in heaven, and there was seen in his temple the ark of this testament: and there were lightnings and voices, and thundering, and an earthquake, and great hail."

The end of the then-known world and the beginning of a new way of seeing truth will begin. The wars will begin to end, natural disaster will begin to end, and the world will begin to come to a true, normal state. Christians and all other religious groups will begin to change for the better. A large number of people will move to the east coast of America. This area of people will begin to govern the ideas of the whole nation.

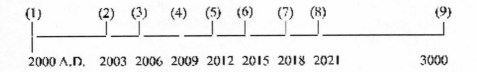

1. The seventh seal began.

The first trumpet sounds 2000, 2001, and 2002.

The twenty years of American good, bad, and grievously bad years.

Economic problems, terrorist attacks, war.

2. The second trumpet sounds 2003, 2004, and 2005

Three years of more problems in America, with the church affairs and morality.

The years of good, bad, and grievously bad years with natural disasters, hurricanes, etc.

3. The third trumpet sounds, years 2006, 2007, and 2008.

The year in which biblical philosophy will be questioned.

The coming of a great teacher in the word of God.

Three more years of good, bad, and grievously bad years with economic problems, terrorist activities, and war.

4. The fourth trumpet sounds 2009, 2010, and 2011.

Three years of the elected of God beginning to awaken from spiritual death.

Three more years of good, bad, and grievously bad years, with natural disasters, hurricanes etc.

5. The fifth trumpet sounds.

A new awaking in moral, social, economic, and political areas. The ideas of the third trumpet will bring a great movement to start in the fifth trumpet.

Three more years of good, bad, and grievously bad years in area of economy, terrorist activity, and war.

6. Sixth trumpet sounds.

Great social unrest and economic changes in America. A change in religious belief for thousands of people.

Three more years of good, bad, and grievously bad years.

More natural disasters and hurricanes, plus heavy fighting in the Middle East, and possibly the United States as well.

7.   The seventh trumpet sounds.

A change in the government of America to a nation with ideas of true justice.

A time when all nations will look within for new ideas for all of their people.

A new beginning; times of good, bad, and grievously bad years will be overcome with unity.

8.   2021 will give new ideas in life for the American people.

Black and white Americans will begin to walk in true equality.

9.   The year 3000 A.D. the Seventh Seal ends.

CHAPTER THREE

THE MYTHS SURROUNDING THE STORY OF JOSEPH

No great figure has ever appeared in history without an abundance of myths and stories growing up around them. Adam and Eve, Joseph and Potiphar's wife, and even Jesus Christ and his mother Mary are no exception. (*Lost Books of the Bible and the Forgotten Books of Eden*)

This writing of Joseph in Egypt has been a very important writing for all students of the Bible. It is a myth; a writing of events that are to happen in the future in a nation as of Egypt. These events in the writing of Joseph will happen around a people who have the bloodline of Joseph in the midst of them. From Genesis 39, we can see the slavery involvement that these people would come into. The name Joseph only identifies the chosen people and a royal bloodline.

Genesis 39:1; "And Joseph was brought down to Egypt; and Potiphar, an officer of Pharaoh, captain of the guard, an Egyptian, bought him of -the hands of the Ishmaelites which had brought him down thither."

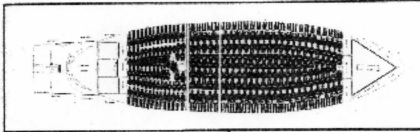

I. *Diagrams of the lower deck of
Vigilante, a typical slave ship.*

When looking into the myth in verse 1 of chapter 39, you can see this nation of America. Before this event happened to Joseph, he was known as the chosen of his father's children, of all twelve. Twelve in this myth represented the total (twelve tribes, twelve disciples, twelve stars, etc.). But in this verse, you should see the word Joseph as the chosen of God Almighty and of a royal bloodline, because Joseph's bloodline will travel through Jesse, David, Solomon, Jesus, and beyond, to the Son of Man (Matthew 1:17, Luke 3:23-28). Joseph was to become a slave to a servant of the king (the Pharaoh). He was to serve the officer of Pharaoh, the captain of the guard, an Egyptian. This meant that Joseph was a servant of servants, in an outpost area (colony) that was an area of the Pharaoh of Egypt. This is the same as the North American slave trade. The slave came from a place where all or total human life evolved from (Africa). They were purchased from the Portuguese traders who were Christians (the new Ishmaelites, or people of God) and sold to the colonies of English landlords (captain of the guard) or servant to the king.

Genesis 39:2-3: "And the Lord was with Joseph, and he was a prosperous man, and he was in the house of his master, the Egyptian. And his master saw that the Lord was with him and that the Lord made all that he did to prosper in his hand."

God has and will always be there with the chosen people, even in the darkest moments. God must protect His word. Although His people were to go through hardship, they also were to come out with great substance. God must protect this people so He can fulfill His words. That is what makes God be God: "The Word." The African slave was a prosperous man or woman to their slave masters. Truly, this prosperity in the life of the slave masters gave them wealth that surpassed some of the landlords of Europe. The slaves lived on the plantation (in the house of his master), the field hands lived in small houses, and the house slave, at times, lived in the master's house to serve him at all times, day or night. The master saw that the Lord had permitted this act of slavery to become a part of his possession. The religious teachings of that time, "the Famous Curse" taught that God had willed the inferior position of the black man. He was to be the "hewer of wood and drawer of water" to his white brother. **Genesis 39:3 "And his master saw that the Lord was with him and that the Lord made all that he did to prosper in his hand -."** This shows how much the Caucasian slave owners saw their slaves as being a great addition to their life, a life that would make some of their lives like kings and royalty.

From the fifteenth century, when Portuguese traders raided Africa and brought the first Negroes to Europe, to the nineteenth century, when the slavery of black men was justified from the pulpits of white American churches; through all that time, Noah's curse was held as proof that slavery of Africans was not a crime against men, but rather, was the will of God Himself. What was this curse? The Bible tells us that the waters of the Great Flood destroyed all the life that was on earth, except for the people and animals who were with Noah in the Ark. When the flood receded and left the Ark high and dry on Mount Ararat, those who were in it emerged, resumed their lives, and began to multiply. Noah had three sons – Japheth, Shem, and Ham – and of them the whole earth over was spread. After the flood, Noah planted a vineyard. The vines flourished; the grapes ripened, were picked, and were pressed into wine. And Noah "drank of the wine and was drunken; and he was uncovered within his tent." Ham entered his father's tent, found him lying naked, and went and told his brothers. The brothers, Shem and Japheth, took up a garment between them and walking backwards into their fathers tent covered him without letting their eyes look upon him. When Noah awoke and learned what Ham had done, he uttered the famous curse: "Cursed is Canaan; a servant of servants shall he be unto his brethren." That is the story as the Bible tells it, and for centuries Bible readers had no doubt about its meaning (*Chronicles of Negro Protest,* by Bradford Chambers).

Genesis 39:4; "And Joseph found grace in his sight, and he served him and he made him overseer over his house and all that he had he put into his hand."

For the master to show Joseph (or the black slave) grace in the midst of being a slave in a Christian nation, the word of God had to be used to justify just cause. This famous curse, for hundreds of years, was made into an excuse for buying and selling blacks into slavery. But how was Joseph helping the master grow in wealth and other areas of his life? This was a time when the slave had a bigger part to play in the life of his master. The better the blacks served the master and his children, the more authority he and she began to have; even today; blacks like Colin Powell and Miss Rice are examples in today's time of American history. All black Americans are in the house of the master and the master's children, trying to move up in life for true equality.

Genesis 39:5-6; "And it came to pass from the time that he had made him overseer in his house and over all that he had, that the Lord blessed the Egyptian's house for Joseph's sake; and the blessing of the Lord was upon all that he had in the house and in the field. And he left all that he had in Joseph's hands; and he knew not ought he had, save the bread which he did eat. And Joseph was a goodly person, and well favored."

The North was blessed by the free labor of the African slave and their children, the South also was blessed with the slaves and large sums of wealth, all of the landlords were happy. Because of Joseph (the black slave) being in America, they all were blessed.

These riches made the United States the nation that had become the richest member of the world powers. The slave became well-favored among the master and his children. The blacks, as time continued, received the Emancipation Proclamation, a declaration to free the slave (humanitarian principle). This declaration gave blacks authority over all things in the master's house (nation); for example, bread (power over money). Although the blacks have risen to different levels of power, the currency is one area the United States whites still control by them-selves. This control left the ex-slave and his children in a position to always depend upon his former master's children for the substance of building a better life. For a house, he must go to the master's children, and the same for cars, for food, for jobs, etc. This power over the blacks will always keep them in a voluntary slavery. When he prays to his God, his substance will come to him through his ex-slave master's children, through all of the above.

Genesis 39:7-23; "And it came to pass after these things that his master's wife cast her eyes upon Joseph; and she said, lie with me. But he refused, and said unto his master's wife, 'Behold my master wotteth not what is with me in the house, and he hath committed all that he hath to my hand; There is none greater in this house than I; neither hath he kept back anything from me but thee, because thou art his wife: how then can I do this great wickedness, and sin against God?' And it came to pass, as she spake to Joseph day by day, that he hearkened not unto her, to lie by her, or to be with her. And it came to pass about this time that Joseph went into the house to do his business; and there was none of the men of the house there within. And she caught him by his garment, saying, 'Lie with me:' and he left his garment in her hand, and fled, and got him out. And it came to pass, when she saw that he had left his garment in her hand, and was fled forth, that she called unto the men of her house, and spake unto them, saying, 'See, he hath brought in an Hebrew unto us to mock us; he came in unto me to lie with me and I cried with a loud voice: And it came to pass, when he heard that I lifted up my voice and cried that he left his garment with me, and fled, and got him out.' And she laid up his garment by her, until

his Lord came home. And she spake unto him, according to these words, saying, 'The Hebrew servant, which thou hast brought unto us, came in unto me to mock me: And it came to pass as I lifted up my voice and cried that he left his garment with me, and fled, and got him out. And it came to pass, when his master heard the words of his wife, which she spake unto him, saying, 'After this manner did thy servant to me; that his wrath was kindled.' And Joseph's master took him and put him into the prison a place where the king's prisoners were bound: and he was there in the prison. But the Lord was with Joseph and shewed him mercy and gave him favor in the sight of the keeper of the prison. And the keeper of prison committed to Joseph's hand all the prisoners that were in the prison; and whatsoever they did there, he was the doer of it. the keeper of the prison looked not to anything that was under his hand; because the Lord was with him, and that which he did the Lord made it to prosper."

Most Afro-Americans that are fifty years of age or older can see this area very clearly, and also others that lived in this time period. This area, Genesis 39:7-23 shows the 1960s until our time today. During the days of the Equal Rights movement, the Black American was about doing his business, wearing his robe of being a person that changed legislation to his advantage, such as Martin Luther King Jr. and other civil rights leaders. This event pressed President Lyndon Johnson to act in behalf of making this nation live up to its word that all men are to be equal. But after Martin Luther King Jr., Malcolm X, and others were assassinated, the Equal Rights Act, as years went on, slowed down with the rise of the ERA women's movement. Here you can see the wife, or Caucasian woman, coming to lay with the black movement by the words of the Equal Rights Act (no discrimination of sex). The women's movement came to life from this ERA, this sex rights or female rights act. Today we can see where the white female has used the legislation to get her and other females out to the front of all other Equal Rights movements. These events have given the black man's garment, or coat, to the hand of the white female. She has become the voice of today, next to the white male. The saying "came in unto me to mock me" shows - that she should be the one in power next to the white male. The white power structure could not see among the black leader the "take-care-of-business" attitude from the black community after the ERA came into power. So the prison system became a part of the black man's life. Many black males and females have come in and out of this system. The scripture shows that this was a plan by the white male to do this. Drug crimes or usage in some nations is a medical problem, but in America, the drug crime and usage in black communities has a very high penalty in the courts. The prison systems have benefited. Some prisons have become privately owned and the stock market has been making money off the system. Tax money, free labor, etc., have been there to help the system and its members make large sums of money.

Martin Luther King, Jr. celebrates 1956 Montgomery bus boycott victory by riding "up front." One result of boycott was King's rise to national leadership.

Chapter 40 of Genesis goes back and gives an overview of the development of the nation of America, from the large colonies of England to America it has become today.

Genesis 40:1-23; "And it come to pass after these things, that the butler of the King of Egypt and his baker had offended their lord the King of Egypt.

"And Pharaoh was wroth against two of his officers, against the chief of the butlers, and against the chief of the bakers.

"And he put them in ward in the house of the captain of the guard, into the prison, the place where Joseph was bound.

"And the captain of the guard charged Joseph with them, and he served them: and they continued a season in ward.

"And they dreamed a dream, both of them, each man his dream in one night, each man according to the interpretation of his dream, the butler and the baker of the King of Egypt, which were bound in the prison.

"And Joseph came in unto them in the morning, and looked upon them, and, behold, they were sad.

"And he asked Pharaoh's officers that were with him in the ward of his lord's house, saying, 'Wherefore look ye so sadly today?'

"And they said unto him, 'We have dreamed a dream, and there is no interpreter of it.' And Joseph said unto them, 'Do not interpretations belong to God? Tell me them, I pray you.'

"And the chief butler told his dream to Joseph, and said to him, 'In my dream, behold, a vine was before me; and in the vine were three branches: and it was as though it budded, and her blossoms shot forth; and the clusters there of brought forth ripe grapes: and Pharaoh's cup was in my hand: and I took the grapes, and pressed them into Pharaoh's cup, and I gave the cup into Pharaoh's hand.'

"And Joseph said unto him, 'This is the interpretation of it: the three branches are three days: yet within three days shall Pharaoh lift up thine head, and restore thee unto thy place: and thou shall deliver Pharaoh's cup into his hand, after the former manner when thou wast his butler.

"'But think on me when it shall be well with thee, and show kindness, I pray thee unto me, and make mention of me unto Pharaoh, and bring me out of this house: for indeed I was stolen away out of the land of the Hebrews: and here also have I done nothing that they should put me into the dungeon.'

"When the chief baker saw that the interpretation was good, he said unto Joseph, 'I also was in my dream, and, behold; I had three white baskets on my head: and in the uppermost basket there was of all manner of baker meats for Pharaoh; and the birds did eat them out of the basket upon my head.'

"And Joseph answered and said, 'This is the interpretation thereof: the three baskets are three days: yet within three days shall Pharaoh lift up thy head from off thee, and shall hang thee on a tree; and the birds shall eat thy flesh from off thee.'

"And it came to pass the third day, which was Pharaoh's birthday, that he made a feast unto all his servants: and he lifted up the head of the chief butler and of the chief baker among his servants.

"And he restored the chief butler unto his butlership again; and he gave the cup into Pharaoh's hand: but he hanged the chief baker: as Joseph had interpreted to them.

"Yet did not the chief butler remember Joseph, but forgot him."

This chapter of Genesis is truly about this nation and its struggle to find itself as a member of England's elite colonies, thriving for their own independence. The butler is the northern part of this country, and the baker is the southern part of the nation. Later, the butler became the Republican Party, and the baker became the Democratic Party. But from the start of this nation's independence, it had offended the King of England.

"And it came to pass after these things that the butler of the King of Egypt and his baker had offended their Lord the King of Egypt."

For over a century after Jamestown was founded in 1607, the colonists went their own ways with little notice from the mother country. North America grew and prospered greatly. This was a time when England was dealing with its troubles at home. The colonies and England grew apart. The North American colonies did little in helping England defeat France in 1763, because the colonists enjoyed a large degree of self-government. Every colony had its own representative assembly, which could put pressure on the governor by threatening to hold back money. The king was offended, and the English tightened their control. British troops also protected the colonists against Indians. This was part of the reason England believed the colonists should share the costs, and so England enforced old laws and passed new ones to raise money.

Genesis 40:2-3; "And Pharaoh was wroth against two of his officers, against the chief of the butlers, and against the chief of the bakers.

"And he put them in ward in the house of the captain of the guard, into the prison, the place where Joseph was bound."

Between 1765 and 1774, the colonists strongly opposed every effort to make them pay more taxes. Then the British Parliament passed the Intolerable Acts. These acts closed Boston Harbor to shipping, which meant economic ruin. It also took back the charter of Massachusetts, which ended local self-government. The dispute had been about taxation; this made the colonies go from self-government to being under a "ward," the state of being under guard. The colonies were under guard in their own land, "the house of the captain of the guard." This was the land where Joseph (the black slave) also lived.

Genesis 40:4; "And they continued a season in ward."

From 1763 until 1775 the colonies did not like the treatment of England toward them. Fighting started in April, 1775. At first, only a few colonists wanted full independence. As fighting went on, the British government was unwilling to give in at all. Finally on July 4, 1776, the Declaration of Independence was signed.

Genesis 40:5; "And they dreamed a dream both of them, each Man his dream in one night, each man according to the interpretation of his dream, the butler and the baker of the King of Egypt, which were bound in the prison."

The northern and the southern colonies had their own agenda. Independence did not lead immediately to democratic government, but it started the wheel turning. The colonies eventually created a republic, a group of separate states, each giving up some governing rights to become united under a central government. But before that had all happened, a Civil War came into play. The dream of the two, "the butler and the baker of the King of Egypt," the north and the south, had their own dreams of controlling the nation and the area in which they lived. Joseph, or the black slave that "served them," heard both of their dreams for greatness; to make the motherland proud of their achievements.

Genesis 40:6-14; "And Joseph came in unto them in the morning, and looked upon them, and, behold, they were sad. And he asked Pharaoh's officers that were with him in the ward of his lord's house, saying, 'Wherefore look ye so sadly today?'

"And they said unto him, 'We have dreamed a dream, and there is no interpreter of it.' And Joseph said unto them, 'Do not interpretations belong to God? Tell me them, I pray you.'

"And the chief butler told his dream to Joseph, and said to him, 'In my dream, behold, a vine was before me;'"

When looking at "they were sad," the Civil War is the reason they were sad. On April 12, Confederate guns fired on Fort Sumter, and the Civil War began. In both north and south, the common men saw the war in a less idealistic way. In the south, it was called a "rich man's war and a poor man's fight." In the north, it was called that, too, and "the nigger's war." Many white working men saw it as a fight for black men who would only become competitors for their jobs when freed. The Union resorted to the draft by 1863 to fill the army's ranks. The enrollment bill went into effect. In New York City, for four days, an anti-draft riot killed twelve hundred people. They attacked police, beat black people to death, burned Negro homes and businesses, and attacked draft offices. There were weak and cowardly men in all nations, and they were among the Americans. A drafted man could buy an exemption for three hundred dollars, or pay a substitute to fight for him. It was so bitterly resented that ninety-eight of the registrars were killed in the first four months of the law. This is written of Genesis 40:6-14, as the chief Butler and Joseph were to see the northern dream of controlling the nation of American lives; and in the myth of the south, or the baker's dream of controlling the nation was to die or be controlled by the North. The time of the Civil War was one of the saddest times in American history; a time when brother fought against brother, and cousin fought against cousin. Almost all families in this nation were affected. The black slaves (Joseph) saw this effect put on his master and their families. Chapter 40 is all about this nation's struggle to power from Jamestown to Washington D.C. This chapter will end its history in about 2000 A.D.

Chapter 41:2-7-15-24 of Genesis is an area that all Bible students should go back to and take a hard look, because this area has the future events of America, from 2000 to 2021, inside its writings. We have been taught by most teachers of the seven years of good harvest and seven years of bad harvest; but to see a clear picture of these events, we must look very carefully at the writing. When seeing this myth, a picture should be drawn of the kine (cow), corn, river, meadow, brink, stalk, rank, good and east wind, etc.

Genesis 41:1; "And it came to pass at the end of two full years, that Pharaoh dreamed: and, behold, he stood by the river."

Here we would see Pharaoh as the ruling party and the top leader in America; President Bush and the very top powerful senators. Two full years would be seen as two hundred years, and the beginning of this new millennium.

Genesis 41:2; "And, behold, there came up out of the river seven well-favoured kine and fattleshed; and they fed in a meadow. And, behold, seven other kine came up after them out of the river, ill-favoured and lean-fleshed; and stood by the other kine upon the brink of the river."

Genesis 41:4; "And the ill-favored and lean-fleshed kine did eat up the seven well-favored and fat kine. So Pharaoh awoke and he slept and dreamed the second time: and, behold, seven ears of corn came up upon one stalk, rank and good. And, behold, seven thin ears and blasted with the east wind sprung up after them. And the seven thin ears devoured the seven rank and full ears. And Pharaoh awoke, and behold, it was a dream."

The dream that the Pharaoh saw was about the future of a nation like that of Egypt, which is the nation of North America, the United States. We, as a people of America, must understand that this writing is to prepare us to survive the trouble that is to come, so some human flesh can be saved. There will be twenty-one years of events that will come. It will start with a good year, a bad year and a grievously bad year. These years will start from 2000 A.D. and go until 2021 A.D. The first three will start with bloodshed and war. The next three will have natural disaster in its path. All three years of bloodshed or terrorist attacks and war will be about the economy. First, a good year, no problem; second, a terrorist attack or bombing; and third, war. These years would be from 2000 to the end of 2002. The next set of three years will be from 2003 to the end of 2005. They will be about natural disasters (corn and east wind) because the corn and east wind is about nature. The first of the second set is to be a good year, 2003; and the second, a bad, 2004 (hurricanes); and the third year of the second set is grievously bad (more hurricanes). Although the pattern will start over with 2006 being a good year from the terrorist attacks, but 2007 will be a bad year, and also, 2008 will be grievously bad. These three-years are about war and blood. Also, when applying the seventh trumpet to this count, they too are arranged in the same sequence as the kine (cow) and corn and east wind. And after 2008, the year 2009 starts the natural disasters again, but remember the first year is to be a good year, the year 2009. Then 2010 will be a bad year for the state of the economy, because of the hurricanes (east wind) and other disasters created by strong winds. The third year of that set will be grievously bad, like the year 2005, but a little worse. These patterns will repeat themselves over and over again. They will get worse each time they are repeated, until America truly becomes the kingdom that God Almighty wants it to be.

To find out how the writer came up with the number of years and the events, we would start from chapter 41:2. "There came up out of the river." The river is about the destiny of Egypt or this nation like it, America. "Seven well favored kines (cows) and fat fleshed," is about the economy and life of the people being good for seven years. "And they fed in a meadow." This is about the state of the nation as a good land to live in, with good growth.

Now in verse three of the same chapter, we would see seven bad kines (cows) coming up after the seven good cows.

"And, behold, seven other kine came up after them out of the river, ill-favored and lean-fleshed; and stood by the other kine upon the brink of the river."

These bad cows are going to stand by the good cows (kines). Now look where they will stand by them; upon the brink of the river. The word "brink" is to be understood in order to see this picture more clearly. "Brink" is defined as a slope; a bank of a river; a point of onset. These cows, good and bad, are to stand by each other on the slope or the bank of the river, from the onset, or start to the top of it. The years these cows represent will start and be good, bad, and grievously bad, seven times, until they get to the top, or the end. This word "brink" is very important to understand in this story.

Now the next part of this picture of the cows is in verse 4 of this chapter.

"And the ill-favored and lean-fleshed kine did eat up the seven well-favored and fat kine. So Pharaoh awoke;"

This, in itself, is another seven years that had not been counted by bible teachers in the past. This is an event of seven years that is to be a part of the other fourteen events or fourteen years. So they are also on the brink of the river beside the bad cows. They are seven years grievously bad, because the bad ate up the good and overshadowed the years.

In the next dream of the corn, we will see the same types of events of years, but only this time, natural disasters will rule the years.

Genesis 41:5; "And he slept and dreamed the second time: and, behold, seven came up upon one stalk, rank and good."

The dream about the corn shows seven years of good, prosperous times. But the word "stalk" is seen as a supporting or connecting part. And "rank" is important to understand, as well . "Rank," in this writing about the corn, is offensively gross or coarse, and also ranged side by side in orderly arrangement. So here, the corn dream shows the seven-year of good, with problems.

Genesis 4:6 "And, behold, seven thin ears and blasted with the east wind sprung up after them."

The seven thin and blasted are bad ears in the king's dream. The word "thin" means having less than the usual number, disappointingly poor or hard. Also, the word "blasted" means damaged by or as if by an explosive, lightning, or wind (New Collegiate Dictionary). The word "blasted" also points to a natural disaster that is a part of these seven ears of bad corn. But "east wind" is also part of the events of these years of corn. There, the east wind sprung up after them. "Sprung" is the past of "spring," which mean "to jump, to move by elastic force, to come into being." So this east wind in the Middle East area was hot, gusty, and laden with sand. It was harmful to vegetation. The wind was recognized as God's creation and was used as an instrument to perform displeasure (Exodus 14:2; Psalms 78:26;148:8; II Kings 2:11) and his judgment (Psalms 48:7; Jonah 1:4). The nation of America has hurricanes as east winds. They are part of God's judgment and displeasure on this nation. God will always do according to his will.

So far, when looking at the Pharaoh's dreams about the corn, we see seven good years with some problems, and seven bad years with hurricanes, or east wind. All together, we see fourteen years with these two events. But there is a third event that is to happen with this corn.

Genesis 41:7; "And the seven thin ears devoured the seven rank and full ears. And Pharaoh awoke, and, behold, it was a dream."

There the full and rank ears will be devoured. This word, "devour," is to seize upon and destroy or consume. So this event of seven devoured years will have the east wind inside it, and it will become the very grievously bad years.

One of the last events to see in this story of the Pharaoh dream is that he awoke.

Genesis 41:7; "And Pharaoh awoke, and behold, it was a dream."

Here we can see that the Holy Bible writing is a book of true magic, showing us the future of our world America and its destiny. "And Pharaoh awoke" shows us that, as time comes to an end of judgment, the leaders of the nations and the world will see that God's movement on America and the world is to be seen through the myths in the scripture of the Holy Bible.

To sum this chapter up, you can see that there will be a nation like Egypt (America) that is to go through a judgment of twenty-one years. Seven of these years are to be good with some problems. Then there will be seven bad years, with war, terrorist attacks and the east wind (natural disasters). Finally there will be seven more grievously bad years, with some wars, terrorist attacks and natural disasters that will overshadow them. These events in the two dreams are as one; that is, they work together.

The first six years shown are a historical fact.

These years are shown as good, bad and grievously bad over and over, from 2000 to 2021. The first set (three years) is first about terrorist attacks and war the second set is about natural disasters. These sets of years will rotate until the twenty-one years are over.

This chart is about the economy in America as good, bad, and grievously bad, showing that this nation is going through a judgment. It gives the events of these twenty-one years.

Kine (cow)	2000	Clinton	President	Good year
Terrorist	2001	Bush	President	Bad year (9-11)
War	2002	Bush	President	Grievously bad (war)
Corn	2003	Bush	President	Good with problems (war)
Natural	2004	Bush	President	Bad (hurricanes)
Disaster	2005	Bush	President	Grievously bad (hurricanes)
Kine (cow)	2006	Bush	President	Good with problems (war)
Terrorist	2007	Bush	President	Bad terrorist (war)
War	2008	Bush	President	Grievously bad terrorist (war)
Corn	2009	Bush	President ?	Good with problem (war)
Natural	2010	Bush	President ?	Bad (hurricanes)
Disaster	2011	Bush	President ?	Grievously bad (hurricanes)

Kine (cow)	2012	Bush	President ?	Good with problems (war)
Terrorist	2013		President	Bad terrorist (war)
War	2014		President	Grievously bad terrorist (war)
Corn	2015		President	Good with problem (war)
Natural	2016		President	Bad (hurricanes)
Disaster	2017		President	Grievously bad (hurricanes)
Kine (cow)	2018		?	Good with problem (?)
Terrorist	2019		?	Bad terrorist (war)?
War	2020		?	Grievously bad (terrorist)(war) ?

This chart and the chart on the seven trumpets are to be used in understanding how the events are to effect the people of America and the world, because almost all nations are connected to America and its economy.

CHAPTER FOUR

TITHES, OFFERINGS, AND TAXES

This is a subject that a large number of religious leaders choose to teach the traditional way, but we must also say that some don't know how to teach it rightly. What is tithe, as learned from the word of God?

Tithe, the Hebrew word asar, "to tithe," is derived from the word signifying "ten," which also means "to be rich." The basic principle in the thing is the acknowledgement that everything rightly belongs to God, including a man's own property and that men are only stewards. The tithe is a token brought to honor the Lord and to recognize Him as owner of all. (*Wycliffe Bible Dictionary*, Charles F. Pfeiffer, Howard F Vos, John Rea Editors).

This meaning of tithes is basic. The history and the use of tithes is better understood in the teaching of the scripture.

Genesis 14:18-24; "And Melehizedek, King of Salem, brought forth bread and wine: and he was the priest of the highest God. And he blessed him and said, 'Blessed be Abram of the most high God, possessor of heaven and earth: and blessed be the highest God which hath delivered thine enemies into thy hand, and he gave him tithes of all.'

"And the King of Sodom said unto Abram, 'Give me the persons and take the goods to thyself.'

"And Abram said to the King of Sodom, 'I have lifted up mine hand unto the Lord, the most high God, the possessor of heaven and earth. That I will not take from a thread even to a shoelatch, and that I will not take anything that is thine, lest thou shouldest say, I have made Abram rich: Save only that which the young men have eaten, and the portion of the men which went with me, Aner, Eshcol, and Mamre; let them take their portion.'"

Abraham is shown as a tithe payer of all goods he had. Whether he was in battle or not, he paid his taxes (tithe). Most leaders teach that this was a religious act, but this was a political, as well as moral responsibility. Melchizedek, to whom Abraham paid tithe (taxes) was the king of the area. This king received from Abraham and others. At that time of history among Abraham and his people the political and religious leadership was one, even in the days of the Leviticus priesthood. So scriptures suggest the amount of the tithes consisting of one-tenth of all yearly produce and of the increase of flocks and cattle (Exodus 23:19). There was also a priestly leave offering; that had been separated (Deuteronomy 26:1).

What does this mean? Tithes, offerings, and taxes are the same. The religious organizations have, for years, received tithing from the people of their fold. The U.S. government had taken tithing (taxes) from the same fold that the religious church have received from. The word has been used to justify the religious organizations reason of this act to receive taxes ("Render unto Caesar what is Caesar's and to God what is God's"). This scripture has been used to teach the church members to pay money to the church because the church money is to be looked at as separate from the government's money. But if America is a nation "In God we trust," then it is not like Caesar's nation, but as the nation of God. And if this is so, then the tax paid to our government is our tithes and offerings. So what are we paying the church? The investment money of many individuals is paid to the church, and when they become old, they are sometimes broke. Many are left to live on social security checks, which is not much. If the churches would demand the money (tax dollars) from the government to help the people of its environment, then our society would become more helpful to all. If America is to be a nation for God the Almighty, then the church must learn to help the people of their fold with their investment money. The church and the state must pass laws that help the people of society, as well as the church environment, have more goods and services for themselves. The judgment is on America to bring about these social and political changes.

Chapter Five

The Prodigal Son

This story of the lost son in Jesus's teaching is about God dealing with Noah's youngest and oldest sons. All throughout the Holy Bible, Noah is shown as having three sons, and the Koran shows Noah as having four sons in the beginning, before the flood. This story is from the days after the flood of Noah, until now and beyond.

Luke 15:11; "And he said, 'A certain man had two sons:'"

When most readers see this saying, they don't know that this is Noah. They think that this man only has two sons. But the story is about an older and younger son. That is the reason the words are written ("A certain man had two sons").

Luke 15:12; "And the younger of them said to his father, 'Father, give me the portion of goods that falleth to me.' And he divided unto them his living."

When reading this, about a father and a son, we should see that Jesus said "Call no man father but God." So this father symbolizes God the Almighty. In this verse, we can see that there was more than one person involved. He (God) divided unto them his living shows that these substances were not just given to one, but to all that were involved. Now we will go to the story of Noah to better understand the beginning of this parable of the prodigal son (Luke 15:11-32), because this parable has been called "the gospel within the gospel" and "the crown and pearl" of all Jesus's parables.

Genesis 9:1; "And God (Father) blessed Noah and his sons, and said unto them, 'Be fruitful, and multiply and replenish the earth. And the fear of you and the dread of you shall be upon every beast of the earth, and upon every fowl of the air, upon all moveth upon the earth and upon all the fishes of the sea; into your hand are they delivered. Every moving thing that liveth shall be meat for you; even as the green herb have I given you all things. But flesh with the life thereof, which is the blood thereof, shall ye not eat.'"

Here we can see where God divided unto Noah and his sons the blessings, and how they should live their life. By God blessing them, the substance of the world was at their hand. Obeying the words of God itself placed them in the position to receive the goods that were to come into their life. Also, we can see in the story of Noah that the younger son was the first to step forward to receive the blessings of goods in moral, political, social, economic, food and appetite areas. These blessings were also extended to you and me, and to all human beings on the planet.

Genesis 9:8-9 "And God spake unto Noah and to his sons, with him saying, 'And I behold I establish my covenant with you, and with your seed after you;'"

Although the blessings are a pledge to you and me , the youngest son is not about every person who is going through troubles. This youngest son is Ham's seed, who will go through the Transatlantic slaves trade in this story. The oldest son will be Japheth, the dad of the European races, head of the gentile nations (Genesis 10:2-5).

Luke 15:12; "And the younger of them said to his father, 'Father, give me the portion of goods that falleth to me.' And he divided unto them his living."

In the story of Noah, we see that Cush, one of Ham's sons, begat Nimrod, and he began to be a mighty hunter before the Lord.

Genesis 10:9-10; "He was a mighty hunter before the Lord: wherefore it is said, even as Nimrod, the mighty hunter before the

Lord. And the beginning of his kingdom was Babel, and Grech, and Accad, and Calneh, in the land of Shinar. Out of that land went forth Asshur, and builded Nineveh and the city Rehoboth and Calah."

Ham's seed was the first to build civilizations and nations, like Egypt and areas in the Middle East.

In the land of Shinar (Genesis 10:10) Ham's seed developed mankind into one language and one speech.

Genesis 11:3-5; "And they said one to another, 'Go to, let us make brick and burn them thoroughly.' And they had brick for stone and slime had they for mortar. And they said, 'Go to, let us build us a city and a tower whose top may reach unto heaven; and let us make us a name, lest we be scattered abroad upon the face of the whole earth.'

"And the Lord came down to see the city and the tower, which the children of men builded."

Luke 15:13; "And not many days after the younger son gathered all together, and took his journey into a far country."

Ham's seed gathered all the people together (Genesis 11:6). There was nothing that they were restrained to do when they had imagined doing it. Their socializing, politics, economy, and diet and appetites were in a higher state than ever before. They had a rich spiritual culture and great scientific wisdom. The astonishing achievements in building and unity surpassed that of the modern world; so much, that God had to intervene and had them to take a journey into the face of all the earth (Genesis 11:7-9).

Luke 15:13 "And there wasted his substance with riotous living."

Here we see that Ham's seed, after being scattered abroad with all others that were with them, began to lose that power of persuasion that brought the people together as one. As time moved on, history shows how a temple was built all over the world. Then, some civilization, as time continued, had vanished. The (disregard of others) step weakened Ham's seed. This disregard of others will be a part of his seed many years to come. It will make Ham's seed become a servant of servants. Even in the day of the Pharaoh, riotous living was so great that the princess of Pharaoh commanded Abram's wife before the Pharaoh. The woman was taken into Pharaoh's house as one of his wives (Genesis 12:14-20).

From the days of Abram coming into Egypt, until the famine that grew in the land (Genesis 12:10), Egypt was plagued with a shortage of real goods or divine guidance. Ham's seed was in need of divine knowledge. Many people of color even today are still in need of knowledge to give them the nourishment to move ahead in life.

Luke 15:15; "And he went and joined himself to a citizen of that country; and he sent him into his fields to feed the swine."

From the time the Greeks came into the control of Egypt until Rome, the Roman people were known as citizens, Egypt became open to the gentile nations. The people who were called citizens in this story that Jesus was teaching are the Europeans who came from the Roman genealogy. They sent the seed of Ham into their fields to feed the swine. Black men, black women, and black children became laborers of the citizen, or the white mass. The black slave of Ham's seed became the "hewer of wood and drawer of water" to his white brother. Simply being a son of Ham caused this so-called curse to come (Genesis 9:19-25).

Luke 15:16; "And he would fain have filled his belly with the husks that the swine did eat: and no man gave unto him."

Here we can see the soul-food diet. This food was not a diet of other cultures, only the slave culture. There was no science in the eating habits of the slaves; it was only to make it taste good. The black slave ate the throwaways from the swine that the master would not eat. Food the animals ate was a part of the slave diet; collard greens, neck bones, chitterlings, pig tails, pig feet, chicken backs, and chicken legs were some of the foods of the slave. The body parts of the animals that the master and his children did not eat were used in the slave's diet.

Luke 15:17; "And when he came to himself, he said, 'How many hired servants of my father's have bread enough and to spare, and I perish with hunger!'"

Ham's seed, the black slave, begins to look into the future for their places in the nations where they had became a servant of servants. In the Christian nations of God, he wanted to have a part of the economic and freedom that the white mass had, because in nations like America there was an abundance of goods and wealth for all who wanted to achieve.

From the desire of freedom, the slaves received their emancipation from slavery. The Confederate and the Union had to put an end to the ownership of slaves. The life of the black slaves of Ham's seed was on the move toward the highest level of freedom.

Luke 15:18; "'I will arise and go to my father and will say unto him, father, I have sinned against heaven, and before thee.'"

The blacks began to be an active part of the religion of the European colonies and the nations of the gentiles. In America, the A.M.E. churches grew, as well as others. The gospel teaching was a shadow over their life that was to deliver them from their grief (Jonah 4:6), and today, the gospel is like a gourd over the head of many black's lives .

In the life of Ham's seed in America, blacks had begun to arise in many ways to become the people God Almighty wanted them to become. The nation of Islam and Elijah Muhammad began to teach the black men to look at the white mass differently than before; that they, as a people, need to be reprogrammed. They have taught the Negroes the importance of pride in race, and to look toward nationalism. Malcolm X was a defender of the philosophy of Elijah Muhammad. Marcus Garvey, before them, had his plan for a black nation. The difference between the two is that the Muslims had been successful where Garvey's work had ended. Martin Luther King's movement played an important part in blacks moving ahead in life.

He became the Moses of today. Martin Luther King Jr. helped poor people have good jobs, live in the neighborhoods of their choice, marry who they wanted, and other freedoms that were not available before. Elijah Muhammad was like the coming of Elijah of the Bible. He helped turn the hearts of the children to their fathers and the hearts of the fathers to the children by teaching the masses of his followers and others that the blacks were the original people of the planet, and that they should understand that their ancestry was of greatness, and that they also must become like their ancestors had been; controlling their own nation and lives.

Luke 15:19; "'And am no more worthy to be called thy son; make me as one of thy hired servants.'"

As the sixties, seventies, and eighties emerged, blacks began to see God's almighty presence in their lives, and that all of these rights the blacks achieved were because the will of God was with the black movement. Although most whites were often against the freedoms that black's obtained, blacks believed this was legal right from the Fourteenth and Fifteenth Amendments, which said that these rights belonged to them. Black leaders knew that all people born in America should be able to achieve equal rights under the constitution of this nation, "In God we trust." The blacks wanted to live the American dream. The Civil Rights Act of 1866 and the Fourteenth and Fifteenth Amendments gave every citizen of the black race protection of freedom from the black codes. It guaranteed equal citizenship rights. And in the sixties, seventies, and eighties these rights were made new again.

Luke 15:20; "And he arose, and came to his father. But when he was yet a great way off, his father saw him, and had compassion, and fell on his neck, and kissed him."

This verse is part of the continual glory of the blacks in the eyes of the world; how they are to learn that these events that have happened in their lives have all been apart of God's plan; and that the myth has foretold of these events that would occur in their life. The Holy Bible is to be a path of understanding of God's true love for these people as the chosen of God Almighty. The books of the Bible are not taught in the knowledge of the myth, but that the myths will become the way of teaching. The teaching of the myth will open Christians and others to the true path of understanding of the word of God. From this knowledge, the kiss of God will be continual in their lives .

Luke 15:21; "And the son said unto him, 'Father, I have sinned against heaven, and in thy sight, and am no more worthy to be called thy son.'"

The seed of Ham in this story is to be seen as the blacks of the transatlantic slave trade. These blacks will began to see that they have been deceived in their understanding of the gospel, and that God wanted them at this time, from 2006 through 2012, to start opening their eyes to divine truth. This will lead to a repented state of mind. They will begin to understand that they needed God's understanding of truth more than ever before. The true path of God with the knowledge of carrying their cross, is very important to their day-to-day lives; that politics are as important as morality, that the economy is important as food and diet; and that society is a must; and that the family must be protected by true political legislation that benefits the poor, as well as the rich; and that there is no carrying thy cross if church and state are separate.

Luke 15:22; "But the father said to his servants, 'Bring forth the best robe, and put it on him; and put a ring on his hand, and shoes on his feet:'"

This area of scripture is the true liberation of these people from the transatlantic slave trade. There are many scriptures that show that the chosen people of the last days (the days we are in today) are to have a nation of their own. This verse says that this son was given the best robe. The robe signifies the power of a king or person of great political power. The verse said, "Put a ring on his hand." That is the social power of a leader to rule this people. Then the verse said, "Put shoes on his feet as well." This is God giving economic power in all levels to this son; the power to control his own banking system and other economic ventures.

Luke 15:23; "'And bring hither the fatted calf, and kill it; and let us eat, and be merry:'"

This verse is an area of scripture that most Christians of today will not understand before the year 2012, or the days when the fourth trumpet sounds. Animal sacrifice was the only sacrifice that God Almighty accepted. The fatted calf was the new day of the Lord. The calf or cattle is showing economic growth in its highest form. Calves were considered a delicacy for the wealthy (Amos 6:4); but here, killing the fatted calf is more about animal sacrifice than the eating of the animals. So when we see the theme "eat and be merry," it means to enjoy the goodness of God in their lives. This younger son and his people are to come into the highest level of prosperity and wealth that God has to offer.

Luke 15:24; "'For this my son was dead, and is alive again; he was lost, and is found. And they began to be merry.'"

This is the time of the beginning of peace; the days of a "promised land as a people." When looking into the writing of Revelation, you can see the theme of a promised land.

Revelation 11:15; "And the seventh angel sounded; and there were great voices in heaven, saying, 'The kingdoms of this world are become the kingdoms of our Lord, and of his Christ; and he shall reign forever and ever.'"

From among these people of Ham will come the Christ that the world has been looking for. He must become a ruler in the land of promise. This shows a time of deliverance, a time that mankind will began to awaken from the great spiritual death caused by the fall of Adam. The human race will be at its end as we know it today. There will be no more races with humanity. People will begin to understand the ways of God Almighty; that if you are ever to be people of God, you must believe in the cross philosophy of Jesus, and that the five points of the cross are mandatory for all people.

Luke 15:25; "Now his elder son was in the field: and as he came and drew nigh to the house, he heard music and dancing."

The elder son of Noah is Japheth, the father of the gentiles, or white race (Genesis 10:2-5). His seed is in the field. To be in the field is to be the ones who are building nations and kingdoms all over the world. History has shown that Japheth's seed is involved with all nations of the world. Their development has caused some nations to grow, and others to fall. The verse said, "and as he came and drew nigh to the house", he heard music and dancing." This is showing that, as the blacks are building themselves into the people that they are to become, a black church, a black nation, and a people of power, their beginning has involved music and dancing. Music is very important in black Americans lives. Some blacks have become very well known through their music. Dancing or motion is another way the blacks have become well known in entertainment. Jesse Owens and Michael Jordan in sports, and many others have entertained the world. Even today, this activity has dominated the life of so many blacks with wealth. Church music is an important part of black culture.

Luke 15:26; "And he called one of the servants, and asked what these things meant."

There will be a new movement among blacks in America to nationalism. They will believe in the ideals of the cross that do not separate church and state. This philosophy will turn young blacks and whites into thoughts of separatism. This will come about because of their new understanding of the myths of the Holy Bible. This will be something that will make the white race wonder why. The myth philosophy will grow among blacks faster than any other people. They will see that the myths are about their lives. For many years, white America and other nations that have been built by Japheth's seed have developed religious beliefs that they have seen to be right. Through the years of this development, if anyone rose up against their beliefs, they were killed or called heathens. Most whites in our day cannot see the Bible taught any other way than the way it is taught every Sunday at local churches. When the gospel that he has learned for hundreds of years has inside powers to raise a dead people, the black man and his family then will come the fullness of the gospel. This is what the eldest son will see, and ask "What do these things mean?"

Luke 15:27; "And he said unto him, 'Thy brother is come; and thy father hath killed the fatted calf, because he hath received him safe and sound.'"

As the myth becomes real in the life of the black church, the changes in beliefs of the teaching of Jesus will grow farther and farther apart. The black church will see that animals are the only things that can be used for sacrifices, because there has been a curse upon them from the beginning of time. The cross teaching will also be a part of the division in the belief of the people.

Luke 15:28; "And he was angry and would not go in: therefore came his father out, and entreated him."

This new doctrine of belief that is understood by the myth will anger the leading white religious leadership in Christianity, when they see that their teaching was only a part of it, and the fullness of the gospel is in the myth. This will be something that most leaders in religion don't want to hear. Finding out that the religious leaders of your nation have kept biblical truth from you, because the mass of them have refused to accept the myth teaching will divide the church. Masses of people will begin to seek knowledge in the direction of the myth. The black church will begin to see their own lives in these teachings of the myth. These things will bring on the anger of the elder son. The righteous whites, as well as blacks, will feel betrayed.

Luke 15:29: "And he answering said to his father, 'Lo, these many years do I serve thee, neither transgressed I at any time thy commandment: and yet thou never gavest me a kid, that I might make merry with my friends:'"

This is saying to us that the white race has carried the teaching of Christianity for a long time, but the teaching of racism was not in the will of God, nor was teaching that white was right and black was wrong. This belief of the gentile's teaching was not the gospel in its fullness. The gentiles are the ones who, for hundreds of years, carried this doctrine that has built nations from their religious crusade. If any were to benefit at this time, it would be Japheth's seed. But God had, from the beginning, already written the future of human life. The human race is a race that Japheth's seed has led for hundred of years. The whites were in front, then the browns, and last, the blacks of the world. This has been the way that Japheth's seeds and his friends have ruled. Although God had called the gentiles to lead, he has also told of the fulfillment of their leadership (Roman 11:15-36).

Luke 15:30; "'But as soon as this thy son was come, which hath devoured thy living with harlots, thou hast killed for him the fatted calf.'"

The son (sun) of God Almighty was to come from Ham's seed, as the story goes. This person that is the light of God or Son of Man is to come from the dead of the deadest, which is the black race. Many seers talk about this person that is a sun (light) and about the "Age of Aquarius" promising a paradise on earth. Biblical prophets and other seers, like Madame Sulvia, Edgar Cayce, Ruth Montgomery, Mary Morel, and Jeane Dixon; prophets modern and ancient, tell of a new world order. Nostradamus, around 1557, was one of many prophets of our day. But the Bible, in the teaching of the myth, opens our eyes to the future more than any other. In this verse, the white leaders cannot see this black man as ever leading him or replacing him as a leader of the free world.

Luke 15:31; "And he said unto him, 'Son, thou art ever with me, and all that I have is thine.'"

Here we see God informing Japheth's seed, or the white race, that this new teaching is for him, as well; that this is a new age for the people; that this elder son and his seed are to be a part of this new movement, because it is for all people to become free, under a world of peace.

Luke 15:32; "'It was meet that we should make merry, and be glad: for this thy brother was dead, and is alive again; and was lost, and is found.'"

Here we see that God Almighty is saying we should make merry. This means that it will be done, for it is God's will for this son (Ham's seed) to rise from the slave trade to be a major player on the world scene; to have a great nation within this great nation of America. This will happen, because it is the future of this nation. So God wants all races to live in harmony with each other. This is the millennium that is to be the age of peace and freedom. God's will is intended for all humans to live in peace, or die in their wicked ways. The individuals that will survive God's judgment will live in a new world order, an age of peace and prosperity.

CHAPTER SIX

MYTHS AND STORIES

From the beginning of time as we know it, there have been myths. But what is a myth?

"Myth (*greek: mythes*): a usually traditional story of ostensibly historical events that serves to unfold part of the world view of a people or explain a practice, belief, or nature phenomenon. Parable, Allegory" (*Webster's New Collegiate Dictionary*).

These parables, or stories, have entreated mankind for hundreds of years. Some of the myths have been of importance, and some have just been to motivate an individual or a group. But we would like to talk about these myths that are in and out of the Holy Bible's scripture. Some of these myths have come into being in our time through people like Edgar Cayce, Jeane Dixon, Madame Blavatsky, Nostradamus, and others.

Most students of the Holy Bible don't study the books as myths, they study them as a story as it is written. We will compare the difference in the two. We will not take these myths from 4000 B.C. until today, from left to right. We will open them up, randomly.

Jesus Ben Joseph (Jesus Son of Mary), from 26 B.C. to about 4 A.D.: This prophet is one of the most important of the entire Bible, from Adam to our day. There are many myths about his teachings and his life. Some of these writings are in the New Testament of the Holy Bible, which is used by the Western world and other nations of the world. Some see him as the son of God, and others see him as a prophet of God and the son of Mary. Others just see him as a wise teacher. But all people in all nations have heard his name. In the writings of the four Gospels, we can see writing that is attributed to him. Jesus himself did not write these events and stories about his life, but we know the gospel writings as Matthew, Mark, Luke, and John. And because he himself didn't write these sayings, and because they are said to be written about seventy years later, this is one of the reasons, along with others, that his parables or stories would be called myths. For example:

Matthew 24:4-31; "'Take heed that no Man deceive you. For many shall come in my name, saying, I am Christ; and shall deceive many.

"'And ye shall hear of wars and rumors of wars: see that ye be not troubled: for all these things must come to pass, but the end is not yet. For nation shall rise against nation, and kingdom against kingdom: and there shall be famines, and pestilences, and earthquakes, in diverse places.

"'All these are the beginning of sorrows, then shall they deliver you up to be afflicted, and shall kill you; and ye shall be hated of all nations for my name's sake.

"'And then shall many be offended and shall, betray one another, and shall hate one another.

"'And many false prophets shall rise, and shall deceive many.

"'And because iniquity shall abound, the love of many shall wax cold.

"'But he that shall endure unto the end, the same shall be saved.

And this gospel of the kingdom shall be preached in the entire world for a witness unto all nations; and then shall the end come.'"

In Matthew, chapter 24, the gospel is showing the same event four times, but in different ways. This event in the chapter was to occur from the days of Jesus's life to the end of the wicked. At the time of the end of this world of evil, the Son of Man, the Christ, is to come and lead mankind into a world of peace. He would be assisted with his angels (other people of like mind).

When looking at this myth of the future, from Jesus's day until now, we can see history unfold itself. Matthew 24:1-14 is the first story of this chapter; Matthew 24:15-22 is the second myth story; Matthew 24:23-35 is the third; and Matthew 24:36-51 was the fourth myth story. These four are about the same events, just told in a different way.

We will examine the first and third myth story of this chapter of Matthew.

In Matthew 24:4-14, Jesus, or the myth, is showing how, as time went on from the days around 4 A.D. until the end of the wicked, the ones that will come in his name will call him the Christ, and because of this, they will deceive many people. This is a historical event. The Roman Catholic Church, in a great council called the council of Nicaea, said Jesus was not only the Son of Mary, but also the Son of the living God. Jesus became divine. Jesus, almost ninety-five percent of the time in his teachings, is called the Son of Man the Christ. A Christ is a messiah, an anointed person who is to crush the wicked of the world and build a nation that will rule all nations. In Jesus's day, this didn't happen. Is Jesus saying here in verse 5 that he was not the Christ, but that would be the person called by him as the Son of Man? As the story continues for the six verses, Jesus tells of years of wars upon wars that will happen after he has gone away. This was very clear through history. From the day of the Jews' uprising until the day that Rome was divided into ten Germanic tribes, the people that were called by Jesus' name have been engaged in wars. Nation rose against nation, and kingdom rose against kingdom. The East Goths (Ostrogoths) and the West Goths (Visigoths), the Vandals, Lombards, Alemanni, Burgundians, Franks, Anglos-Saxons, and others were at war. These groups were partly nomadic, herding their flocks and tilling the soil. These people prized strength and courage in battle. They worshiped many Gods, including Tiw, the God, of war; Wotan, the chief of the Gods; Thor, the God of Thunder; and

Freya, the goddess of fertility. Their names are in the English words Tuesday, Wednesday, Thursday, and Friday (*History and Life, The World and Its People; 2nd Edition*).

Even today, the idea of these European myths are woven into the teachings of the gospel so deeply that some of the truth has been oppressed to the point that it has lost its value.

These wars are known as a time of tribulation. Jesus tells of a time that the divine path to build a true nation and kingdom of God Almighty by these people who were chosen to carry his name will fall into conditions of famine and pestilence. This is to fulfill the writing in **Amos 8:11-13; "'Behold, the day come, saith the Lord God, 'that I will send a famine in the land, not a famine of bread, not a thirst for water, but of hearing the words of the Lord:**

"'And they shall wander from sea to sea, and from the north even to the east, they shall run to and fro to seek the word of the Lord and shall not find it. In that day shall the fair virgins and young men faint for thirst."

These days will become the "Day of sorrows" (Matthew 24:8), because many men and women will be killed, even by the Catholic Church. The church wanted to control the world of the Christian, and the Pope was seen as the all-seeing eye of God, the God-Man on earth, the Pontiff.

Matthew 24:9-10: "Then shall they deliver you up to be afflicted, and shall kill you: and ye shall be hated of all nations for my name's sake. And then shall many be offended, and shall betray one another, and shall hate one another."

In the time of the Inquisition, the Catholic Church had many people killed as witches, as in the story of Joan of Arc, a simple country girl who had a vision and believed that she heard the voices of saints calling on her to rid France of English soldiers. The words of Martin Luther, a German priest, became an important document. The document of Martin Luther attacked the sale of papal indulgences, which freed sinners from punishment after death. Martin Luther and others felt the Church of Rome abused this practice. His movement began the great movement called the Reformation. The Protestant

Reformation believed that there could be no reforms without major changes in church law. This would lead to the Protestant Church. The events of the Reformation had ties to political and social conflict. Kings and others used religious differences to gain political ends. The medieval period had been an age of faith. It was a time when wars were fought to prevent any one nation from becoming too strong.

Luke 24:11-12; "And many false prophets shall rise, and shall deceive many.

"And because iniquity shall abound, the love of many shall wax cold."

There have been many teachers since Jesus' day, and in our own time, as prophets, and to some of their followers, as a type of Christ. They had came into all races, each seeing their man as the messiah who was to come, or just as the prophet of the hour. John Calvin, born in 1509, was a French lawyer and scholar. He had to flee from France because of his Protestant ideas. Luther had inspired him. He also disagreed with Luther on certain matters. Predestination was an important idea for Calvin. It meant that God had already decided who was to be saved and who was to be damned. Calvin's idea was in a famous book called *The Institutes of the Christian Religion*. Calvin set up a theocracy in Geneva, controlling not only church affairs, but also politics, education, amusements, and family life. Calvin taught that hard work, moral living, and thrift were to be Christian virtues. Moral life and wealth were looked upon as signs that a person was predestined to salvation. The Swiss Reformed, Dutch Reformed, and the Presbyterian Church that were begun by John Knox in Scotland all set up base on the Calvinist model.

In the 1800s, there came prophets like Joseph Smith, leader of the Mormon Church. There are two major groups that come under his name: the Reorganized Church of Jesus Christ of Latter Day Saints, and The Church of Jesus Christ of Latter-Day Saints.

Joseph Smith - History 1:11-20; "While I was laboring under the extreme difficulties caused by the contests of these parties

of religionists, I was one day reading the Epistle of James, first chapter and fifth verse, which reads: If any of you lack wisdom, let him ask of God, that giveth to all men liberally, and upbraideth not: and it shall be given him.

"12 Never did any passage of scripture come with more power to the heart of man than this did at this time to mine. It seemed to enter with great force into every feeling of my heart. I reflected on it again and again, knowing that if any person needed wisdom from God, I did; for how to act I did not know, and unless I could get more wisdom than I then had, I would never know; for the teachers of religion of the different sects understood the same passages of scripture so differently as to destroy all confidence in settling the question by an appeal to the Bible.

"13 At length I came to the conclusion that I must either remain in darkness and confusion, or else I must do as James directs, that is, ask of God. I at length came to the determination to 'ask of God,' concluding that if he gave wisdom to them that lacked wisdom, and would give liberally, and not upbraid, I might venture.

"14 So, in accordance with this my determination to ask of God, I retired to the woods to make the attempt. It was on the morning of a beautiful, clear day, early in the spring of eighteen hundred and twenty. It was the first time in my life that I had made such an attempt, for amidst all my anxieties I had never as yet made the attempt to pray vocally.

"15 After I had retired to the place where I had previously designed to go, having looked around me and finding myself alone, I kneeled down and began to offer up the desires of my heart to God. I had sincerely done so, when immediately I was seized upon by some power which entirely overcame me, and had such an astonishing influence over me as to bind my tongue so that I could not speak. Thick darkness gathered around me, and it seemed to me for a time as if I was doomed to sudden destruction.

"16 But exerting all my powers to call upon God to deliver me out of the power of this enemy which had seized upon me and at the very moment when I was ready to sink into despair and abandon myself to destruction not to an imaginary ruin, but to the power of some actual being from the unseen world, who had such marvelous power as I had never before felt in any being - just at this moment of great alarm, I saw a pillar of light exactly over my head, above, the brightness of the sun, which descended gradually until it fell upon me.

"17 It no sooner appeared than I found myself delivered from the enemy, which held me bound. When the light rested upon me I saw two Personages, whose brightness and glory defy all description, standing above me in the air. One of them spoke unto me, calling me by name and said, pointing to the other - This is My Beloved Son Hear Him!

"18 My object in going to inquire of the Lord was to know which of all the sects was right, that I might know which to join. No sooner, therefore, did I get possession of myself, so as to be able to speak, than I asked the Personages who stood above me in the light, which of all the sects was right (for at this time it had never entered into my heart that all were wrong) and which I should join.

"19 I was answered that I must join none of them, for they were all wrong; and the Personage who addressed me said that all their creeds were an abomination in his sight; that those professors were all corrupt; that "they draw near to me with their lip, but their hearts are far from me, they teach for doctrines the commandments of men, having a form of godliness, but they deny the power there of".

"20 He again forbade me to join with any of them; and many other things did he say unto me, which I can't write at this time. When I came to myself again I found myself lying on my back, looking up into heaven. When the light had departed I had no strength; but soon recovering in some degree, I went home."

This story is the root of the Mormon Church belief. And for over a hundred and seventy years, there have been many souls following this belief. They have came from many nations of the world, with their hearts and family, into the workshop of this prophet's teaching. The state of Utah has been developing because of the followers of this prophet. So who was this man that came in the name of God in the last days? Was he a true prophet, or was he a guru to mankind? These are questions the true followers of Jesus and God Almighty must ask themselves. Because in the book of Ezekiel the Son of Man is told.

Ezekiel 13:2 "Son of Man, prophesy against the prophets of Israel that prophesy and say thou unto them that prophesy out of their own hearts, hear ye the word of the Lord;

"Thus saith the Lord God; Woe unto the foolish prophets, that follow their own spirit, and have seen nothing! O Israel thy prophets are like the foxes in the deserts.

"Ye have not gone up into the gaps, neither made up the hedge for the house of Israel to stand in the battle in the day of the Lord.

"They have seen vanity and lying divination, saying, the Lord saith: and the Lord hath not sent them: and they have made others to hope that they would confirm the word. Have ye not seen a vain vision, and have ye not spoken a lying divination, whereas ye say, the Lord saith it; albeit I have not spoken?

"Therefore thus saith the Lord God; Because ye have spoken vanity, and seen lies, therefore behold, I am against you, saith the Lord God. And mine hand shall be upon the prophets that see vanity and that divine lies: they shall not be in the assembly of my people, neither shall they be written in the writing of the house of Israel neither shall they enter into the land of Israel; and ye shall know that I am the Lord God."

This writing in the book of Ezekiel about understanding the Son of Man, and whether prophets are true or false, is also for the people of God, as well. Joseph Smith could have been a true prophet or a guru. The way to find out is to understand the prophecy. If the prophecy points to Joseph Smith, then, and only then, can you say he was true. The writing of Doctrine and Covenants, section 113, answers certain questions about the writing of Isaiah, given by Joseph Smith, the Prophet, March 1838.

"1. Who is the stem of Jesse spoken of in the first, second, third, fourth, and fifth verses of the eleventh chapter of Isaiah?

"2.Verily thus saith the Lord: It is Christ.

"3.What is the rod spoken of in the first verse of the eleventh chapter of Isaiah, that should come of the stem of Jesse?

"4. Behold, thus saith the Lord: It is a servant in the hands of Christ, who is partly a descendant of Jesse as well as of Ephraim, or of the house of Joseph, on whom there is laid much power.

"5. What is the root of Jesse spoken of in the tenth verse of the eleventh chapter?

"6. Behold, thus saith the Lord, it is a descendant of Jesse, as well as of Joseph, unto whom rightly belongs the priesthood, and the keys of the kingdom, for an ensign, and for the gathering of my people in the last days."

This writing, in Doctrine and Covenants 113, was supposed to have been given to the prophet Joseph Smith at Far West, Missouri, April 17, 1838. Some Mormons teach that this person who is to hold this priesthood and the keys of the kingdom, as an ensign, and for the gathering of God's people in the last days, was Joseph Smith himself, and that this person was of the descendant of Jesse, as well as of Joseph. So the big question is, was Joseph Smith the Son of Man, or a prophet, like Elijah? Was the Son of Man a person who would come through the Mormon Church at a time when blacks were not allowed into the priesthood? These are question you must ask yourself, because the writing said that this descendant of Jesse and Joseph rightly belong to the priesthood, with the keys of the kingdom. The mythical writing of Joseph in the book of Genesis in the Holy Bible shows that he must have come through the transatlantic slave trade. History has shown that the people of that group were rejected the priesthood by the Mormon Church (LDS) until the late seventies and early eighties.

Jeane Dixon was a lady in America history who had prophesied the assassination of Robert Kennedy, the shooting of Martin Luther King Jr., the Apollo-Saturn 204 disaster, Lyndon Johnson's withdrawal from the presidential race, the coming of the child from the east, and many other things. In the book *Jeane Dixon, My Life and Prophecies*, as told to Rene Noorbergen, it is said, "In her late forties, a successful real estate broker, she has no reason to want to seek the limelight of publicity, for her life has been fulfilling enough ever since her psychic gift came to the surface. Ambassadors, statesmen, presidents, businessmen all seek her advice, and many foreign dignitary prefers to have an appointment with Jeane Dixon instead of a private reception at the White House. Her reputation has reached far beyond our shores." (*Jeane Dixon, My Life and Prophecies*)

The prophecy that we will look into is about the Child from the East. This is one that most resembles the Son of Man who is to come.

Jeane Dixon

THE CHILD FROM THE EAST

A revelation that was given me on the morning of February 5, 1962, and partly reported in *A Gift of Prophecy*, foretells one of the most dramatic events in the history of the world.

If our world is "a lesson book for the universe", as some have said, then the event that is foreshadowed in this prophecy should be one of the most instructive chapters in the history of Man.

Invariably, at the termination of my speeches, when I indicate my desire to answer listener's questions, people ask me for more details regarding the child that was the focal point of this prophecy.

"When", "they ask", "will we hear more about him? Where is he now? When will he make his appearance on the world scene?" I feel the time has come to report the revelation in its entirety.

It began on the evening of February 2, 1962, when, while meditating in my room, I became aware of a curious phenomenon. The lights grew dim, and as I looked up at the chandelier I noticed all five bulbs darken, except for a curious round ball of brilliance which glowed in the center of each. It did not last long. In fact, I recall thinking that it was probably caused by some defect in the electrical system. Jimmy felt the same way and both of us forgot about the "light failure" until the same phenomenon reoccurred the following evening.

Again I was meditating, seeking our Lord. This time the light faded out a second time, leaving only those brilliant globes of light within. How much time elapsed exactly I do not know- perhaps ten seconds-but I suddenly became cognizant of a tiny crackling sound emanating from inside the globes. When the crackling sound ceased, the lights returned to normal. I then began to sense something was happening over which I had no control. When however, the performance was repeated in exactly the same manner on the third evening, I knew that an event of tremendous importance was about to be revealed to me. I then realized that the phenomenon of the lights was a prelude of things to come. I went to bed confident that God would let me know if and when I was to receive this revelation. He did.

It happened early the following morning, on the fourth day, when I awoke and walked toward the east window of my room, preparing to greet our Lord with the twenty-third psalm on my lips. I gazed out my window and although the sun was still in hiding, what I saw was almost beyond description. The bare-limbed trees of the city had given way to an endless desert scene, broiled by a relentless sun. Glowing like an enormous ball of fire, the sun had cracked the horizon, emitting brilliant rays of scintillating light, which seemed to attract the earth like a magic wand. The sun's rays parted, facilitating the appearance of an Egyptian Pharaoh and his queen. I immediately recognized her as Queen Nefertiti; the Man with her I took to be her husband, reported by history to be Ikhnaton, the so-called "heretic Pharaoh". Holding hands as lovers do, they emerged from the brilliant rays, majestic in their bearing; Ikhnaton's royal headdress was a sign of his power under the sun... not of power under the Son.

But my eyes were drawn to Nefertiti and the child she tenderly cradled in her other arm. It was a newborn baby, wrapped in soiled, ragged swaddling clothes. He was in stark contrast to the magnificently arrayed royal couple.

Not a sound broke the unearthly silence as they issued forth with the child. I then became aware of a multitude of people that appeared between the child and me. It seemed as though the entire world was watching the royal couple present the baby. Watching the baby over their heads, I witnessed Nefertiti hand the child to the people. Instantly rays of sunlight burst forth from the little boy, carefully blending themselves with the brilliance of the sun, blotting out everything but him.

Ikhnaton disappeared from the scene. Nefertiti remained. I observed her walking away from the child and the people, into the past, into the secret past of the ancients. Thirsty and tired, she rested beside a water jug, and just as she cupped her hands to drink, a sudden thrust of a dagger in her back ended her life. Her death scream, piercing and mournful, faded out with her.

My eyes once more focused on the baby. By now he had grown to manhood, and a small cross, which had formed above his head, enlarged and expanded until it covered the earth in all directions.

Simultaneously, suffering people of all races, knelt in worshipful adoration, lifting their arms and offering their hearts to the Man. For a fleeting moment I felt as though I were one of them, but the channel that emanated from him was not that of the Holy Trinity. I knew within my heart that this revelation was to signify the beginning of wisdom, but whose wisdom and for whom? An overpowering feeling of love surrounded me, but the look I had seen in the Man when he was still a babe-a look of serene wisdom and knowledge-made me sense that here was something God allowed me to see without my becoming a part of it.

I also sensed that I was once again safe within the protective arms of my creator.

I glanced at my bedside clock. It was still early - 7:17 a.m. what does this revelation signify? I am convinced that this revelation indicates a child, born somewhere in the Middle East shortly after 7:00 a.m. on February 5, 1962 - possibly a direct descendant of the royal line of Pharaoh Ikhnaton and Queen Nefertiti-will revolutionize the world. There is no doubt that he will fuse multitudes into one all embracing doctrine. He will form a new "Christianity", based on his "Almighty power", but leading Man in a direction far removed from the teachings and life of Christ, the Son.

In this writing, we can see that Jeane Dixon saw a great leader who was to come on to the scene in our time. She goes on to say that the birth of the child had too many similarities to the birth and the life of Christ to be mere coincidence (pg. 187 of *Jeane Dixon, My Life and Prophecies*). She said that the circumstances surrounding the birth of the "Child from the East" and the events I have since seen taking place in his life make him appear so Christ-like, yet so different, that there is no doubt in my mind that the "child" is the actual person of the Antichrist, the one who will deceive the world in Satan's name. His life will be seen to be an imitation of Christ's life on earth.

When we examine Jeane Dixon's story on the "child" the Bible is a good book to use. She calls this child an Antichrist that was very Christ-like. Could she have seen the Son of Man coming and not understood who he was? The timing of the childbirth in her prophecy was very important. She was convinced of the revelation that she saw and that 7:17 a.m. on the clock had something to do with his birth. Could it be that he was seven years of age at the time she had this revelation? Some scholars of the pyramid of Cheops teach that an Egyptian king will come around 1954, and that he will also rise to a new level of mind by 2002. Could this be the Son of Man who is in Daniel 9:25-27? The writing of the pyramid could be found in the book (*Secrets of the Great Pyramid* by Peter Tompkins, pages 15, 75, 93, 114, 115, 217 and other pages). The teachings of Daniel 9:25 and Romans 11:25 shows us that this Man of God should come at the end of time as a deliverer of mankind. Jeane Dixon could have seen him and did not understand who he was, because he was so much like the spirit of Jesus, his descendant. The scripture speaks of this great man and his genealogy coming out of the East and living in the West where some people called eagles are (Roman, European), and also a carcass people (dead of themselves, black America), as in Matthew 24:27-28. It is easy to see this black leader coming from a poor black community, and not the Middle East. Jeane Dixon's timing of the great leader with the cross philosophy could well be the Son of Man.

Michel de Nostradamus wrote of this person who Jean Dixon and others had seen. The writing of Nostradamus could be found in John Hogue's 1997 book, *The Complete Prophecies*.

Epistle to Henry 1; "...At the eve of another desolation when the perverted church is a top her most high and sublime dignity... there will proceed one born from a branch long barren, who will deliver the people of the world from a meek and voluntary slavery and place them under the protection of Mars...The flame of a sect shall spread the world over...

Here again, we see this leader on the scene with the teachings of a deliverer. His teachings spread over the world like the Son of Man. The Bible teaches of him delivering the saints of the most high. The Bible also shows that the people will be learning a false belief about the word of God (Amos 8:11-14). Today many Christians have overlooked the true teachings of the cross philosophy. Without this teaching, the gospel is taught in part.

C4Q50; "Libra will see the Western lands [America] to govern; holding the rule over the skies and the earth no one will see the forces of Asia destroyed until seven hold the hierarchy in succession."

Nostradamus sees the leader as a Libra born in October of the year 1954. This is the time that the pyramid prophecy said the person of the king's chamber should be born. Here we see him in America, growing into a leader. Also at this time, Asian (Middle Eastern) forces will be a problem for America. We can see the area of Asia being a problem, even now.

C5Q79; "The sacred pomp will come to lower its wings. At the coming of the great legislator, he will raise the humble, he will vex the rebels, none of his like will be born on earth."

Here again, the religious leader is involved in legislation in and out of the church.

Matthew 24:30-31; "And then shall appear the sign of the Son of Man in heavens, and then shall all the tribes of the earth mourn, and they shall see the Son of Man coming in the clouds of heaven with power and great glory.

"And he shall send his angels with a great sound of a trumpet and they shall gather together his elect from the four winds, from one end of heaven to the other."

The church as we know it today will be changed. The Son of Man will teach the fullness of the gospel. The elected people of God will follow this leader as America goes through the judgment handed down by God. These individuals will overcome the troubles that will confront America now and in the near future.

C2Q28: "Second to the last of the prophet's name will take Diana's day [the moons day] as his day of silent rest, he will travel far and wide in his drive to infuriate, delivering a great people from subjection."

Nostradamus shows this person as a deliverer many times in his writing. There he shows something about his family; that he would be next to the last person in his family. The last person, his young brother, will have the name of a prophet.

The reference to the first line of Quatrain 28, Century 2 also seems to infer that the new spiritual leader has a name related to the moon. For example the word Diana could be changed to Artemis. With the word Artemis, you can get the name **Armstr**ong. When placing the name over each other you can see the word moon.

Artemis	Lewis	
Lewis	Jer**ome**	
	Armstr**ong**	**Moon**

Diana resembled the Greek goddess Artemis. If you take the letters in the name "Artemis" as Nostradamus has his reader do, you can see the person's name.

C2Q29; "The Man from the east will come out of his seat passing across the Apennines to see France, he will fly through the sky, the rain and snow and strike everyone with his rod."

Nostradamus sees this person flying in an airplane in the year 1994 in the area of France. He also sees what he was doing on the plane. That he will change seats on the plane. Nostradamus shows him as a man that will travel in all types of weather conditions.

C5Q84; "He will be born of the gulf and unmeasured city, born of parents obscure and shadowy: he who the revered power of a great king, will wish to destroy through Rouen and Evreaux."

Nostradamus said the spiritual leader will be born in an area of a gulf and unmeasured city. This means he would be born in the state of Florida on the East Coast, in a city across from the Gulf of Mexico. Nostradamus is also saying here the leader that is to come from parents who would be of a dark race and very poor. But he will grow up to be admired profoundly as one of the greatest leaders of history. Nostradamus goes on to say he will appear as a king to many people. Could Nostradamus be saying there will be a powerful black president in the near future in America?

In these and many other writings, Nostradamus wrote about this leader and others. Could this Michel de Nostradamus be the Michael of Daniel 12:1-3?

Daniel 12:1-3; "And at that time shall Michael stand up, the great prince which standeth for the children of thy people: and there shall be a time of trouble, such as never was since there was a nation even to that same time: and at that time, thy people shall be delivered, everyone that shall be found written in the book.

And many of them that sleep in the dust of the earth shall awake, some to everlasting life, and some to shame and everlasting contempt.

And they that be wise shall shine as the brightness of the firmament; and they that turn many to righteousness as the stars forever an ever.

In the writings of Daniel, we see this person called Michael standing up or raising the prince's awareness of self. Then he will become the leader of God's people in a time of great trouble. The event of his coming marks what we know today as the ending of time. After the years of trouble, there will come a great age of peace and happiness.

Edgar Cayce is another prophet who has seen future events that will occur in America in our time. Cayce is called, by some, an American prophet.

The *New York Times* once named Edgar Cayce "the most fascinating man in America." Despite having only an eighth-grade education, he was called on by world leaders (such as Woodrow Wilson), prominent scientists (such as Thomas Edison), and Hollywood producers to advise them on their most pressing problems. Treasure hunters, stockbrokers, and oilmen made millions of dollars from his talents, while he himself lived much of his life in poverty. In a hypnotic trance so deep he was twice pronounced clinically dead, he diagnosed illnesses with astonishing accuracy and prescribed medical treatments that were years ahead of their time, curing people with life-threatening diseases (*Edgar Cayce an American Prophet* by Sidney D. Kirk Patrick). There were other writers who had told of Edgar Cayce seeing a leader as of a superman who would come among the black race in America. This prophecy has a biblical term about it. Could that person he saw be the coming Son of Man?

Helena Petrovna Blavatsky was a seer who had seen the coming of a spiritual leader who would bring in a new consciousness in our age. Madame Blavatsky was, from 1831-1891, a psychic and a prophet. She is known as one of the leading psychic seers of the nineteenth century. Madame Blavatsky predicted that the Maitreya would appear in Asia around the year 1950. Nostradamus's equivalent of Blavatsky's prophecy occurs in quatrain 50, century 4. Madame Blavatsky, as well as Jeane Dixon, believed in Asia as the home of the new world leader. Unlike these two Nostradamus seen the religious/ political leader coming out of the western nation. Both believed in this person as being a religious leader, also.

September 24, 2003

Dear Mr. President

I am Minister Lewis Jerome Armstrong who has a gift of understanding prophecy. I am also in Nostradamus writing.

I believe Mr. President that You and Your administration are in Bible prophecy. This is a time of humanity history so it is very important to understand the true meaning of the prophecies.

In the Holy Bible the book of Luke the eleventh chapter starting from verse 29 through 36 is a area in which You can be identify. President Bush Your activity as acting President and Your family name is found in the Book of Luke 11:33. The word Bushel has your family name inside it. Bush is located inside. Bushel identify the person. You Mr. President that will be in power in the West. Mr. President Luke 11:32 says that You would go to war with Iraq and also Luke 11:31 says that You will go to war with Saudi Arabia. God has placed a great responsibility on Your shoulder. Mr.

President after Your next term Your brother in Florida
may be President.

   In the writing of Luke 11:29 – 30 a door is open to
show our present time of humanity history. When using
the prophecy of Jonas Mr. President, the Bible can
show You and Your administration the insight of God
will for this Nation. Jonas suggest to the administration
of Assyria the things that could happen. Mr. President
this is a serious time for our Nation and the
International World. The Holy Bible has many areas
to show past present and future history of this Nation and
other areas of the world. Some of these prophecies have not
been revealed as of today. Mr. President God has given
me a special gift and I am concern about our Nation.

                    Thank you

ABOUT THE AUTHOR

Lewis Jerome Armstrong was born in Florida in a religious family. When he was a child, about twelve years of age, he was told that he would be gifted in the knowledge of God and will travel a great deal promoting that truth. He was given a great mind to struggle for the path of true enlightenment. Mr. Armstrong was educated in high school and college in the state of Florida. Business administration and building were things he liked to do. Since he was a child the thought was ever-present in his mind he said "I was born to be a leader". Leadership in the knowledge of the Holy Bible scripture and other books of prophecy influenced his life greater than any others. This book, "Black Nostradamus Prophecies of America's Future", is the book Mr. Armstrong is hoping all Americans and others will read.